Kassie,
Thanks for
years of ff
Jay Musfeldt
2006

ECHOES
Reflections of a Hometown Heritage

Written and
Illustrated
by
Jay N. Musfeldt

Copyright © 2006
Jay N. Musfeldt

All rights reserved. No part of this book may be reproduced in any form, except for the inclusion of brief quotations in a review, without written permission from the author or publisher.

Jay N. Musfeldt
563 Tierra Dr., N.E.
Salem, Oregon 97301-4861

ISBN 0-9779924-0-3

First printed April 2006

Additional copies of this book are available by mail.
Send $21.00 each (includes tax and postage) to:
Manning News Journal Publishing
422 Ann Street
Manning, Iowa 51455

Printed in the U.S.A. by
Manning News Journal Publishing
422 Ann Street, Manning, Iowa 51455
1-712-655-3526

DEDICATION

This book is dedicated to the memory of
my mother, Ida Musfeldt, who taught and nurtured
and my dad, John Musfeldt, who could really tell a story.

Special thanks to:

My wife Julie for reading, encouraging,
and critiquing all those years,

My children Melissa and Robert for listening
to my 'way back when' stories,

My friend, Pam Kusel, whose labor and expertise
enabled *Echoes* to become a reality.

*In loving memory
of that little family,
Mom, Dad, Jay, Bets, and Phil
who shared those exciting years
in that old house out on the farm.*

Table of Contents

The Cloze is Froze 1
A Man of His Time 4
Thanks a Lot, Alexander 5
The Lady on the Street 7
Springtime is a State of Mind 9
The Very Last One 11
Someone is Interested 13
The Plague 15
A Bang or a Whisper 17
Good for What Ails You 19
We Got our Money's Worth 20
Manning's Mechanical Marvels 22
Five at a Time 23
Elmer's Garage 25
A Scentimental Journey 27
From the Heart 29
Food of Memory 31
The Men Wore Hats and the Women Wore Dresses 33
Keep Your Eyes on the Sky 35
Forecast, Cold! (Part I) 37
Forecast, Cold! (Part II) 38
The Rites of Spring 40
It's Polka Time 42
The Longest Day of School 43
What Did You Say? 45
In Good Hands 47
Out the Kitchen Window 49
Our Cottage Industry 51
A Midsummer Night's Misery 53
Not Really Fall 55
M-O-O-M-M! What's There To Do? 57
When is a River Not a River? 59
You Can't Get There From Here 60
If These Bricks Could Talk 62
It's All About Caring 64
Hello From Omaha 66

Bringing in the Chickens	68
The Very First	70
Crickets in the Hay	72
They Got the Job Done	74
Who Knew it Would be Valuable?	76
How Many Ways?	78
It Doesn't Get Any Better Than That	80
Under One Roof (Barns I)	83
Except in Winter (Barns II)	85
Here's to You, Howard Cosell	87
A Basketball Town	88
A Fine Line Indeed	90
You Know it's Spring	92
Some of my Best Memories Are Smells	94
One Man's Foolishness	96
My Little Train	98
No One Lives There Anymore	100
Spring Thaw, Country Style	102
The Golden Globe Reward	104
You want What for Christmas?	106
We Must Have Been Out of Our Minds	108
A New Little World	111
Not Lately	113
Watch Your Fingers	115
We Had One	117
Let's See What You're Made Of (Heritage I)	119
To Each His Own (Heritage II)	121
Back in the Grove	123
If Mupps was Here	125
It Must Be About Time	127
The Great Window Painting Contest	129
A Word of Thanks	130
Picture Perfect	132
Now That Was a Winter	134
They Did it All (Rural Schools I)	136
The Colors of Fall (Rural Schools II)	138
A Fine Beginning (Rural Schools III)	140
We Were a Little Family (Rural Schools IV)	142

The Cloze is Froze

It definitely was no laundromat - that is for sure. There are lots of little things that folks today take for granted, but none is less thought of than the automatic washer and dryer. Doing the wash is not much of a task today. I mean, all you have to do is shove the dirty stuff in the hole and push the button. Drying is even less of a deal. You push the wet stuff in another hole, push another button and that's it. The toughest part is making sure that you've hit the right heat setting on the dryer so that your family wardrobe doesn't come out the size of doll clothes and that your permanent press doesn't appear with permanent, baked-in wrinkles. You take 'em out, fold 'em, and that's "wash day."

Back then, it was a different story. Now we're not talking about pounding out the dirt on a rock by a stream or scrubbing away with a washboard (although the washboard was not dead by any means for hand washing a few things). We are, however, dealing with a time when "wash day" meant just that, a full day's work.

You could count on it. On Monday mornings every clothesline in Carroll County was in use. That's just the way it was done. After a weekend of slightly less work than weekdays, wives rose early to "tool up" for the weekly task of keeping the family presentable.

So far, most of the tasks required for the job were pretty recognizable. The clothes were rounded up from wherever Papa and the kids normally put them. Usually one trip through the various rooms and past the clothes basket got most of the articles. A quick trip outside was sometimes needed to bring in Papa's hog vaccinating overalls or cow barn cleaning coveralls which had been banished to the clothesline to air out.

The first hurdle was to find the washing machine. Especially in farmhouses, this was not as ridiculous as it seems. Until the early '50s, lots of farm houses did not enjoy the luxury of hot and cold running water which is a prime requisite for modern washers. Those farms therefore did not have nice, heated laundry rooms to make the task more civilized. The family wringer washer was likely to be found anywhere from the basement, if you were lucky, to the back porch, or even in another building entirely - the wash house. Dating to the era of gasoline engine and foot pedal-powered Maytag's, the wash house also had fulfilled the need for a means to obtain hot water. Often a wood burning stove heated the big copper boiler for a couple of hours before the washing task actually began. This method of heating water was not limited to wash houses. Kitchen ranges often were the heat source for the copper boiler in homes without wash houses. This created an atmosphere not unlike a tropical rain forest. If you've ever experienced this on a July day, you can begin to understand the logic behind a separate building called a wash house.

The time lag created by heating the wash water was used profitably for other tasks. In some homes, this time was used to carve coffee mug sized cakes of homemade lye soap into smaller chunks that would dissolve in a reasonable amount of time in the washing machine. Though disappearing in the '50s, the practice of making the family's washing soap by boiling beef fat with lye was not yet an unknown procedure. While soap making is another whole story, suffice it to say that homemade soap could cut through just about any grime that Papa or the kids could grind into their Osh Kosh or Big Smith's. It could also do a real job on a woman's hands. Next time you wash clothes, a moment of silence and a nod in the direction of the Tide and Cheer factories might be in order.

Once hot, the water was transferred, one bucket at a time, to the tank of the wringer washer. The clothes that were lightly soiled were washed first; this previous hot water had to last for more than one load. Talk about environmentally gentle! A skillful housewife could do a whole day's wash with less than 50 gallons of water. In an era when water was pumped by a windmill into a cistern for use by the family and livestock, this was extremely important during hot summer days with no breezes.

While the first load is washing, a damp rag was used to wipe the clothesline. In the summer you fought the birds, and in the winter the cloth froze to the wire clothesline. What fun!

Next it was time to rinse, wring, and get the first load to the line. There were elements of a race at this point. Some women took pride in being the first in the neighborhood to get the clothes "on the line." Not that they drove around and checked, mind you, but a peek down the road or over the back hedge...

Hoping that it wouldn't rain, no trucks would go by upwind on the rural gravel road and the birds hadn't found the ripe mulberries yet, the dutiful wife hung the clothes on the line. With real luck, a brisk breeze came up and the clothes dried nice and soft.

Not so in winter. It was a real job, lugging a basket of wet sheets through the fresh snow to the clothesline where in a short time they were frozen stiff as a board. As a child, I remember carrying frozen "long-johns" into the house with delight in the fact that they would stand against the wall by themselves or could be stacked like plywood on the kitchen table. A couple of hours over the clothes rack behind the heating stove and whatever moisture that hadn't "freeze dried" on the line was eliminated. A full day's work indeed!

The thump, thump of our automatic washer provides rhythm to my typing. We can wash and dry clothes with almost no attention to the machines that have made our lives easier. No copper boiler, no clothesline, and no wringer. Thank goodness. I'll never forget the time I put my fingers through the wringer of that old Maytag. Ever hear the phrase, "Put through the wringer?" No wonder Mom used a stick to push the clothes in there.

A Man of His Time

His hands moved steadily and surely, like those of any skilled craftsman. As they wove the fibers in and out, aided by the tapered willow peg (He said willow worked best.), his fingers created a pleasing pattern.

His was a refined and necessary art. The need for his visit to our farm was created by a kink, a sharp edge on a pulley, or perhaps a careless tractor operator who didn't hear the cries of "Whoa!" and nearly pulled the track mounted hay carrier through the back of the barn before the big hay rope snapped in two.

The hay rope, an inch thick and perhaps 200 feet long, was essential to hoisting hay into the barn and moving it to the back of the hay mow. It was not as big as a tractor or as intricate as a baler, but with a broken hay rope, the harvest came to a halt. Such a length of heavy rope was expensive; so there was only one thing to do – call Mr. Pratt, the rope splicer.

While the hay making crew laid off for the rest of the day, this farm boy watched with fascination as that quiet man wove the frayed ends of the torn rope into an amazingly thin, extremely strong splice that withstood many more seasons of haying. There were no knots involved. He utilized his knowledge of how ropes were made and wove the broken ends together in such a way that the splice actually became stronger as tension was applied.

Mr. Pratt was a craftsman of his time. There probably isn't much call these days for a person who knows how to splice a rope. Rope splicing is one of those skills which was important at one time but is now almost regarded as folk art. Mr. Pratt, along with "Jap" Ward, who dehorned cattle, 'Hannes Bunz, who could sharpen a plow share with a forge and hammer, and Lou Stamp, the windmill repairman, applied their skills to tasks that were part of a now bygone era.

The rope splicing man tried to show me that day how he did it, but my one lesson wasn't enough. The closest I ever got to rope splicing was making a knotless rope calf halter under the tutelage of my Win or Grin 4-H leader, Gene Wiese. I'm proud of that skill, which I can still perform if I want to. Perhaps, by so doing, I, like the FFA students who went through the exercise of twisting a rope in the old high school gym, retain a bit of my heritage. It's the heritage of a rural people who created, repaired, and used the most basic of tools to survive and fashion for themselves, their families, and their communities a life on the rolling western Iowa hills.

Thanks a lot, Alexander

I swore I'd never get one. Whenever I encountered one of those blasted things I got annoyed. It all seemed rather rude. When I want to talk to someone I want to talk to some "one" not some "thing." My whole concept of etiquette was offended. When the phone rings, someone's supposed to answer it! If I wanted to talk to a machine, I'd get out my tape recorder! There's no way I'm getting an answering machine!

I said the same thing about a computer. Well, as I now sit at my computer typing, our new answering machine hangs on the kitchen wall. It takes a while to convince me of the value of some of these newfangled gadgets, but when I'm sold, I'm sold.

How strange it seems that in our day we are so filled with human contact that we must devise mechanical and electronic means to keep the world at bay long enough to steal a few minutes of peace and quiet. How strange, indeed, that entire households are gone from home so much of the time that contact with one of these people must be accomplished through the leaving of electronic messages to be retrieved when someone finally returns. How interesting it is that our time is so precious today that we're only willing to make one attempt to contact another person, and when that attempt proves futile we mutter to the dead and uncaring telephone, "Why don't they get an answering machine like everyone else?"

When the first telephone lines were strung to farm houses in the rural Midwest it was a different story. The modern complications and annoyances of the telephone couldn't be foreseen. One simple concept stood out - the end of isolation.

It wasn't that friends and neighbors were so far away. Most family members lived within a few miles of one another. The problem was that those were gravel or dirt roads. Miles were longer under those conditions.

There was also the problem of emergencies. A building fire or medical emergency meant running, driving, or riding to the nearest source of help. Lives and property were indeed lost to the clock as even the fastest help sometimes came too late.

Enter the beginning of instant communication - the party line. The first step in the process of linking together the voices of people over a wire was the party line. Half a dozen or so neighboring houses or farms were linked together on a single telephone line. How did folks decide who should answer the phone when it rang? Simple. Everyone knew their ring. Our ring was one long ring and three short rings. Eischeid's was one long, two shorts, and one long. So it went throughout the party line. There was even a "line call." One certain ring pattern was reserved as a general call or emergency call. When the line call ring was heard, it was usually important, and every household sent someone to pick up the receiver and listen in to the announcement. And so the news got passed. When my father was injured while loading cattle onto a truck, Hib Eischeid beat the medical personnel to our farm and proceeded to do our evening chores. The word came over the party line.

There were some hazards and inconveniences for sure. It seemed sometimes that every time you wanted to make a call someone else was already on the line. If that was a real difficulty, a polite, "May I use the line, I have to make an important call,", usually did the trick. Folks seldom got offended by such a request.

In addition, there were those who enjoyed picking up a bit of news by "listening in" on others' conversations. The annoyance level went up quite a bit at this point, depending on the frequency of such activity. A question like, "Irma, did you hear someone pick up a receiver?" often had the desired effect: a quick and anonymous "click" as the receiver went back on the hook.

Of course today's telephones don't have receivers, or hooks, or even cradles. We communicate by means of pokes and beeps instead of cranks and rings. Most of today's phones don't even ring, they sort of warble. We've even decided that the number and type of phone calls we receive require that our calls be screened as to who is calling and whether or not we wish to answer that person's call at all. The telephone has moved to the position of necessary annoyance.

... But not back then. We could hear a friend's voice from miles away "just like they were in the same room." It was possible to take five minutes and check on Grandma's health or the daily prices on the "interior Iowa and southern Minnesota hog markets." The fire in the barn or the farm equipment accident didn't strike quite the same fear now that help was a phone call away. And the quiet (or boredom, depending upon your age) of the farm house evening would never be quite the same after..."That's our ring; I'll answer it." ..."No I will!"... "No I will!"... "M-o-m-m-m!"

The Lady on The Street

I bought my "Buddy Poppy" from the lady on the street.
I tied it on my button hole like the grown up folks I'd meet.
It didn't cost too much, a mere few cents as I recall;
A little price to pay for taking part like one and all.

I don't think that I understood too much what it was for,
Except that my few cents would help someone hurt in the war.
But that was good enough for me and made it worth the dime,
Because my childhood growing up was at a certain time.

All of us kids knew of The War, and some remember when...
You see, 'twas less than ten years back since V.J. day had been.
Our older friends and neighbors told of times from World War I,
While younger men recalled Korea's horrors, barely done.

We knew that World War I had shortened Heinie Hansen's breath.
The Honor Roll named families, so many touched by death.
We knew that Orren's shrapnel wounds would follow him all time;
And so it seemed most natural for me to spend that dime.

Back then it was so natural because so many men
Who wore the poppies proudly knew firsthand what war had been.
War number two was still so fresh; the wounds had scarcely healed
For all those Midwest fam'lies working factory, store, and field.

The little crimson flowers sprouted up and down the street,
As people bought them gladly from the ladies on the street.
Those evenings stand so clearly out in memory today
That every certain Saturday was always Poppy Day.

Today the times have moved so far, and memories are lost
Of darker days and fearful nights and battle's awful cost
And those old wars are all just history in younger minds.
Today the financiers and such fight wars of different kinds.

It's easy to assume that life has always been like this.
With only "little" six-month wars to mar our peaceful bliss.
So stories must be told to keep us all in mind of those
Who paid a lifetime price so freedom would have room to grow.

It's nice to see that little symbol still gets passed around.
The little crimson poppy still is worn in my hometown.
A spot of color, red as blood, reminding those we meet
Just like it did when I bought mine from the lady on the street.

How quickly and terribly times change. Since this piece was written in October 1997, our nation has seen the horror of 9-11 and now struggles with the pain of young Americans again off to war in another land. The remembrance of wounded and disabled veterans now assumes renewed significance.

Springtime is a State of Mind

We've taken the tree down and sent it to the recycling station. The fallen needles have been vacuumed and the decorations stored. The wrapping paper, boxes, ribbon, and other trimmings have gone by way of the garbage. The last few holiday foodstuffs and treats have either been eaten or molded away. We've seen about all the college football games we can stand for one year. So now what do we do for the next three months until spring?

Break out the seed catalogs - what else!

Bless those wise souls at the seed companies. They really know when to mail their catalogs. Just about the time we think that the prospect of facing the next three months, the "dog days" of winter, will send us completely around the bend...Gurney, or Stark Brothers, or Henry Field come through once more.

It has been so for many years. When I was a boy on the farm, the Earl May or Henry Field seed catalog was our primary source for garden seeds. Sure, there was an Earl May store in Carroll, but in the late 1940s and early '50s that drive was not made as easily or as often as it is now. Besides, those minutes or hours spent with the seed catalog were like a mini trip to a new season. If you closed your eyes for a few seconds you could almost smell those blooming lilacs on page 23. Somehow the sight of those perfect Jonathan apples on page 14 stirred the urge to grab the spade and head for that empty space down by the brooder house. The carrots, beans, radishes, and peas on pages three and four had us trembling with the anticipation of spring planting.

There is one other activity which can lift the spirits and draw thoughts toward spring nearly as well as looking at the seed catalogs - especially for men. The Sears store is in the same shopping mall as the drug store where I often have prescriptions filled. The man said my prescription would be ready in a few minutes. I think he did that on purpose. The Sears store has moved its yard and garden equipment right next to the door that separates the two stores, 50 feet from the prescription counter. I think they did that on purpose. Sears and my drug store are in cahoots.

I mean, what else is there to do while you're waiting for your prescription to be filled? Oh, the beauty of shiny, painted steel! Oh, the perfume of new tires and lubricating oil! Oh, the music of those poetic words - "14 Horsepower," "Mower Deck Included," and "No Payments 'til May!" If one looks down the aisle, one can see other men gazing at a piece of garden equipment as if it were the Biblical "pearl of great price." The aroma of new-mown grass and new-tilled soil seems to float through the air on this mid-winter evening.

It's only a wild guess, but I'll bet that more than one new piece of farm equipment began its journey in a dealer's showroom on just such a mid-winter day. Perhaps the farmer went in to just pick up a part for the manure spreader and was taken in by the sight, the feel and the smell of a new John Deere "B" at Puck Implement. We might wonder if those sights and smells carried home to the farm kitchen as the farmer explained to his wife, "The old one is just about worn out anyway."

I hadn't received a seed catalog for years until two innocent acts changed my whole winter. In the spring of 1996 I bought a "famous name" roto-tiller. If you've ever been on this company's mailing list you know they never give up. What I didn't know was that the "famous name who never gives up" company sells their mailing list to a whole bunch of "seed companies you've never heard of" that want to sell you garden seeds and fancy gadgets to help them grow.

The second innocent act was to order a set of organic gardening pamphlets advertised on our local public television channel. I learned they sell your address to any seed and gardening companies the tiller people left out. I've given away more seed catalogs this year than my neighbor did zucchini (page 6) last summer.

They'll probably stop sending the catalogs after a couple of years when they realize I'm not going to order anything. On second thought, perhaps I will order a packet or two of seeds just to keep the catalogs coming. It's a really cheap mid-winter vacation.

The Very Last One

Let's have a little quiz. What was the original purpose of that pipe rail that stands along south Main Street on the east side of the city park? I'll give you a clue - it's probably the last one of its kind in Manning. Don't know yet? Here's another clue - those pipe "fences" used to be common along Main Street and adjoining side streets. The last ones I remember seeing ran along the north side of Fourth Street from Hank Peters' tavern (alias the Corner Café) east to Hoffmann's lumber yard and west from McDonalds (now Duckwalls) to Thrifty Food. Another stood on Main Street in front of the old Struve Motor building. Adults leaned against them and visited. Small children used them as "monkey bars." Older kids walked along the top of them. Give up?

Before one-way traffic and even before Main Street became the exclusive domain for the automobile, it was used by horses, and since horses don't have parking brakes or ignition switches, they had to be tied to ... "Hitch Rails." Manning's city park is likely one of the very few with a genuine, original, bona fide hitching rail. When the last horse was hitched there I don't know, but it's probably been a while.

For the first few decades of its existence, Manning was a horse and buggy town. Farmers and city folk alike depended on horses for machine power, freight hauling and personal transportation. Even though we have passed the year 2000, evidence of Manning's horse and buggy history is still visible. Perhaps along some downtown sidewalks or curbs you can still see where the old hitching rails were anchored. A bit of research will reveal that more than one detached garage in Manning began its existence as a horse barn or a carriage shed. Certainly the width of the older streets in town was originally scaled not to the needs of cars or trucks, but to wagons and their teams of horses. The Noon whistle sounding from the top of the water tower called farmer and team home for dinner in those quieter days before noise abatement ordinances, enclosed cabs and growling engines.

A long-time symbol of Manning's horse and buggy era was a lovely iron sign that for years identified the home of Doctor Smith on Third Street across from the water tower. That sign has probably long since disappeared into history along with the doctor's horse and buggy it represented.

I dimly remember as a child seeing the barn stalls full of big draft horses and mules. I also remember the day the truck came and loaded up all but King and Queen, that last brown team, and departed to places unknown. For years after the full mechanization of Iowa farms, rural pastures still hosted scattered teams of work horses, kept by their owners for sentimental more than practical reasons. Occasionally, one of the old, high-wheeled wagons stands discarded in a grove, and horse-drawn cultivator wheels frame driveways and hold up hanging plants.

All these reminders - the horse collar mirror frames and single trees which adorn the walls of city houses, the pictures in Manning's centennial book, the horseshoes nailed decoratively over garage doorways, and the bits of broken leather, buckles, and brass rings which hang dusty and unnoticed on rusty nails on barn walls - pay tribute to the time when Manning was a horse and buggy town.

Someone is Interested

The 30-something preschool teacher held up the odd children's toy so that the label with the words "Big Button" could be seen. "Oh, that must be why they call it that." She and an assistant had been trying out the toy, purchased at a garage sale. The operation was easy, once you got the hang of it. Two people each grabbed an end of the five-foot loop of nylon cord. After twirling the whole business, jump-rope style, for a couple of seconds, rhythmic tugging on the two ends would set the plate-sized plastic disc spinning, its built-in whistles humming merrily.

Right at this point, the 50-something school principal observed that, had he thought of marketing such a thing, he'd be a rich man. After all, wasn't this just a big, plastic version of the toy his mother had taught him to make as a child?

Yes, a piece of string and a button had served more than once as a diversion to pass the time of an otherwise uneventful evening in a childhood farm house. That was before television provided instant entertainment at the twist of a dial. That was before each supermarket had its "impulse rack" of attractive but worthless plastic dinosaurs, doll combs, and disposable flashlights right by the checkout counter. That was back when some of the most interesting toys weren't purchased at the store, but crafted from fairly simple materials found in most homes and farmyards.

Having grown up in such a time, yours truly nearly made a complete fool of himself (luckily thought better of it) by stopping in traffic to pick up a bundle of shingles that had fallen from some vehicle and was now lying in the middle of a busy intersection. That bundle of shingles would have provided the materials for hundreds of copies of a toy my father showed me how to make. It consisted of a four-foot or so stick with about an equal length of string tied to one end. On the loose end of the string a knot was tied. This was the launcher or catapult for an arrow made from a cedar shingle. The shingle was carved into the shape of an arrow with the head on the thick end of the shingle and the feather end being thinner. A notch was carved in this arrow silhouette right behind the head. With a bit of practice, the knotted string end would be hooked into the notch; and with a flick of the stick, that arrow could be sent sailing for perhaps 50 yards or more. This might not be an appropriate toy for a suburban backyard, but it was great for a farm. After teaching this process to a couple of fourth grade acquaintances, I was assured that it indeed worked just fine. Their mothers suggested I might tailor my teaching to less hazardous activities.

    I tried for many years, but I never could make a decent willow whistle like my Grandpa Musfeldt used to make for us. Perhaps that's where the important point of this whole idea lies. Our family, like our rural neighbor families, didn't have a lot of money to spend on "impulse" toys. Certainly, Santa brought gifts of toys to our house as to others, but we often played with toys that were made for us by parents or grandparents. Those toys also instilled in us the creativity to experiment with designs of our own from time to time. It may be that this sharing of skills was one of the most valuable things our parents and grandparents ever did for us.

    Times are surely different now. The horseweed lances, corn husk dolls, baked mud sculptures, corncob shuttlecocks, and ash limb bow and arrows were made with materials and tools not always available today. Maybe the charm of all these things lay not in the cleverness of the toys themselves, but in the fact that at some point, someone sat down, took some "quality time" and shared a bit of their life with a child.

    I'd like to issue a challenge to you. Don't let opportunities to share a bit of your own life and heritage with a child pass by. Whether it's toy making, needlework, gardening, or how to make tomato jam, it's worth passing on. You might be surprised to find that someone out there is interested in learning what you know.

The Plague

Every year they came. Sweeping out of the North in brown, dusty clouds, they invaded the peaceful countryside. Striking first in one neighborhood, then another, the fearful throng brought curses to the lips of farmers and struck terror into the hearts of farm wives. They altered travel plans, wash days, and rural school recess periods. What plague could possibly disrupt the lives of such hardy rural folk to such an extent? Locusts? Army worms?

No. Gravel trucks.

It was the late '40s and early '50s. The only paved roads in the area were the main highways: 30, 71, 141, and 59. The other "all weather" roads were gravel surfaced, and every so often they would have to be re-graveled. The gravel was hauled to needed areas by a fleet of gravel trucks. These were standard, six-wheel trucks mounted with wooden hopper boxes that emptied from the bottom. Piloted by owner-operators, these machines raced back and forth at breakneck speed from the gravel pits at Lake View to the area being resurfaced.

The trucks weren't really very big. But this was barely at the dawn of the diesel era. Pre-World War II autos were common on the roads. Indeed, Earl Singsank was still driving his Model A Ford to work. In such a time, it was pretty awesome to see a 1950 Ford V-8 loaded with gravel coming at you, traveling 50-plus on a narrow, rural road.

Re-gravelling was viewed with mixed emotions by rural residents. To farm families, that gravel road was freedom. It allowed trips to town, livestock shipments, and feed deliveries in almost any weather. Compared to those rutted, treacherous, and occasionally totally impassable dirt roads, the gravel roads were a Godsend.

But all this came at a price. As the trucks blasted down the rural roads in a cloud of dust, farm wives raced to the clothesline to salvage what they could of the day's wash. Farmers nervously watched hilltops as sons and daughters moved cumbersome farm machinery slowly to and from fields. Mothers kept constant eye on playing children and pets, lest they stray onto the road and into the path of one of the speeding trucks.

Some said the operators got paid by the load, and that's why they drove so fast. Some saw them as outlaws - wild young vagabonds intoxicated by speed and power. Some just said they were crazy.

But to pre-adolescent farm boys, those truckers were the true Knights of the Road. We knew them all: the GMC's, the Dodges, the Internationals. We remembered from season to season the stylish black Chevy stubnose, the snarling Ford V-8's, the chunky red Diamond T. Ah, what heroes! What we'd have given to trade places as the drivers, with arms nonchalantly draped out windows and cigarettes dangling from their lips, raced full bore down the OCO. toward Bill or Hugo Vollstedt's pickup. At the drop of a flag they tripped the belly doors of the hopper boxes, skillfully spreading their loads of wet gravel; and without even breaking speed, they waved and raced back to the lake for another load.

As quickly as they had come, they vanished – off to do another stretch of road. The rural neighborhood returned to normal. Tablet page drawings of the glamorous machines were lost in the back of school desks. Farmers inventoried losses of careless, road-roaming chickens, and the Vollstedt's road grader smoothed and leveled the newly surfaced roads to smooth perfection. All became peaceful as before.

...until next year... when the roar of distant engines would again bring housewives hurrying to clotheslines murmuring softly under their breath, lest their children hear, "I hate those -------- things."

A Bang or a Whisper

Some things go out with a bang, others with just a whisper.

As time passes and brings change to our lives, some things that are accepted as normal one day, seem to disappear in a flash on the next. One Saturday morning in the '50s, there was a fire station and library standing about where the Plaza is now. By 10 o'clock that evening, bang, all that remained was a smoldering pile of rubble following the sudden fire. One day Manning High School stood on South Main Street and Highway 141. In a matter of days, ominous cracks appeared in the structure, and bang, the old high school building was no more. How quickly things can change.

Other things, however, change slowly. In fact, it's not as though there is a big, memorable event that causes the change, but one day we realize, "Wow, what ever happened to the ------? I haven't seen one for years."

When I'd come to town as a young farm boy, there were two activities I'd watch with fascination – the washing of windows and the lowering of awnings. It didn't take much to amuse me in those days. I remember watching the Main Street merchants from the front seat of our old Studebaker. They took these tasks very seriously. Every summer morning Herb Groteluschen, Pete Hansen and others would step out to the front of their stores and crank their canvas awnings into their proper places. Then the washing would begin. I remember watching Bruno Thompson wielding brush and squeegee on the windows of the tavern. Window washing is still with us, but it's been a while since I saw anyone crank out an awning.

It was about 1956 when I saw my last gypsy wagon on the OCO. The single horse-drawn wagon was headed north through the Nishna bottom near the old Hagedorn farm. My parents said that at one time they were quite common, and indeed I do remember three or four wagons coming through during harvest season when I was very young. It seems that the gypsy men were trying to do some horse trading with my dad and some neighbors. Nothing really spectacular happened. One day we realized that the wagons and their nomadic passengers were just gone.

One thing that is very noticeable to a returning native is the disappearance of fences around Iowa fields. Once upon a time, building and repairing fences was part of the day-to-day routine of farm life. I guess there just isn't any need for them anymore. Farmers don't raise as much livestock as they used to, and the corn stalks aren't likely to run away...

Some changes are both quiet and explosive - both sudden and gradual. Such was the case with a miracle called the Salk vaccine. Many will remember the horror that struck the hearts of parents when the first case of Polio (or Infantile Paralysis) was diagnosed each summer. City swimming pools would close and children would be warned to stay away from crowds and water. The fear of Polio was greater for people in that day than the fear of AIDS is today. AIDS is seen as kind of a remote threat to most people, but Polio, that killer and crippler of children struck at random and without warning. Everyone knew someone who had been afflicted. There was the painful walk and withered limb .... "He had Polio as a child, you know."

I remember the big "Iron Lung" that stood in the lobby of the Crystal Theater as part of a fundraising campaign for the March of Dimes. That huge metal can became a permanent home for children and young adults when their respiratory system was destroyed by Infantile Paralysis. In retrospect, the Iron Lung was a horrible fate, but it was the best we had. The Iron Lung, the forearm-clamp crutches and the metal leg brace were all symbols of a merciless disease that struck during the heat of each summer, a time that is supposed to be filled with fun and play.

And then we heard about Jonas Salk and his wonderful research. His Salk vaccine was not the final answer, but it was a beginning. As many of my generation received, with some real fears on the part of our parents, those first three injections, the end of the scourge came into view.

We don't hear much about Polio anymore. It has quietly faded from our consciousness. Those fears of summer have disappeared in a whisper. Some of those quiet disappearances were real blessings.

Good for What Ails You

The sight of the can and the odor were like a breeze blowing directly out of the past. "No kidding! I didn't know they still made this stuff!" The man running the booth smiled and assured me that the Watkins Company did indeed still produce and market this steady selling product which many knew so well – Petro Carbo Salve. Talk about all-purpose; that brown, sticky, pungent smelling substance was used with equal confidence in the cow barn or in the kitchen. It was good for burns, scrapes, cuts, and whatever else might have been in need of a little disinfectant and a lot of tender loving care.

At least that's what Herb Riesselman, that purveyor of Watkins products and good humor, might have told you. Herb was "the Watkins man" for our area. Traveling from farm to farm in that old black Chevy station wagon, he was one of the standard fixtures of rural life, the door-to-door (or was it farm-to-farm) salesman. During a time when farm families went to town much less frequently than now, all sorts of products were sold by door-to-door salesmen. Watkins, Raleigh, and Fuller Brush were some of the most enduring of the home sales companies. The featured lines of products ranged from hand soap to gun oil, mops to vitamin supplements, shampoo to hog barn disinfectant, and even soft drink concentrate.

Joining these salesmen on the rural roads were the feed salesmen. Moorman, Purina, and Wayne were but three of the companies competing for the farmer's feed dollar. Offering a good joke or two, premiums (a set of chisels for a certain number of pounds purchased), genuine interest in the welfare of the farmer, and an equal interest in making a dollar, these gents pitched their products to the farm market. "Say, John, what are you feeding those hogs now? We've got a 12 percent that will get 'em up to 200 faster than anything else on the market." "Ida, just try some of this lotion on your hands, doesn't that smell nice?"

Depending on the day, the state of mind, or past performance, the reception ranged from "Looks like Carl Peterson (the Moorman man) coming down the hill," to "Can't get anything done because of those damn feed salesmen!" Yet, by combining a dash of showmanship with neighborliness and business sense, the door-to-door salesmen managed to make a living on the miles and miles of gravel roads in western Iowa.

It wasn't quite the same, but yes, I did buy a small can of Petro Carbo Salve from the man in the booth, just for old times' sake. And, yes, it still worked as well on my son's skinned base-stealing knees as it did for my John Deere exhaust pipe-burned arms many years ago.

We Got Our Money's Worth

Following Children's Day, the coming of the carnival was the biggest summer event in Manning. For some years, Royal United Shows brought a few evenings of glamour and excitement to the streets of Manning. At a time when Saturday night already meant busy sidewalks and brisk trade to Main Street businesses, the bright lights, side show barkers, and lively music from the carnival rides were the frosting on the community cake. Alleys and side streets were packed with parked cars to the point where folks actually had to walk several blocks to get to Main Street and the grocery stores. Volunteer firemen with flashlights were kept busy moving traffic and filling up makeshift parking areas like the vacant lot next to Ross' Ford Garage.

To an early adolescent farm boy, this was the ultimate in excitement. With a few dollars of strawberry picking money in my pocket and wearing my good clothes, I was ready to head out into the world of the high rollers. Filled with my youthful confidence and optimism, I was sure those glittering prizes on the racks of the "Pitch Till You Win" and "Milk Bottle Toss" booths were just waiting for me to step up and win. Let the others spend their money on rides and refreshments; I would invest my money in activity that held potential for real reward.

In due time, reality began to rear its ugly head, and I understood that the friendly folks operating those easy games didn't make their living by giving away all those fancy prizes to every farm boy who laid down a dime. (A similar lesson was re-learned at a Chuck-A-Luck stand in Templeton a few years later, but that's another story.)

With the end of the strawberry money in sight, it was time to take in the sights of the midway. It was time to watch the older guys try to impress their dates by ringing the bell on the pole with a mighty blow of the sledgehammer. (They always claimed the "carney" had a control that would make it impossible to ring the bell, thereby avoiding the need to give away prizes.) It was time to hear the barker vaguely describe the wonders to be seen in the "burley-cue" tent and then speculate with the other under-age fellows what really went on in there. Some of the guys claimed to have peeked under the tent to see, but they wouldn't tell, so nobody believed them.

The evening reached its finale when our family met to watch the free stage show. Before Ed Sullivan and MTV there were the stage shows, the era's staple feature event of carnivals and fairs. Perhaps the last bastion of vaudeville, these shows featured roller skating duos, trampoline and aerial artists, tap dancers, and animal acts; all performing to the lively tunes dished out by the lone organ player or, in a "really big show," by a small band. It didn't matter if all the performances weren't up to Ringling Brothers standards or if the musicians would never play Carnegie Hall, they truly were "live, right here on our stage."

Perhaps it was there (sitting on a bench in the street between the popcorn stand and J.M. McDonald) that I developed my love for outdoor entertainment and got the itch to perform. Those carnival variety shows were the most polished live entertainment that many of us rural and small town Iowans saw until we left home and ventured into the wide world. The best part of the whole show was that after spending all our money on food, rides, and cheap prizes, we still went home happy with the feeling that we'd truly gotten our money's worth.

Manning's Mechanical Marvels

I've heard that some folks are seeking information on the possible whereabouts of the old popcorn stand that occupied the First National Bank corner for many years. One can tell how long ago that was by realizing that at one time it was possible to buy both "dime bags" and "nickel bags" of fragrant popcorn from the blind proprietor, Mr. Parrish.

While the popcorn stand was a wonderful part of Manning's past, and the search for it is an intriguing task, I'd like to suggest a couple more items for resurrection – Manning's Mechanical Marvels.

One of these marvels was fastened to the brick building by the entrance to Lyden's Studio and Harold's Jewelry. (The bolt holes were still there last time I looked.) It may have been the only vending machine in town at that time. The faded letters read, "One cent delivers a tasty chew." By depositing a penny, a child could watch the little figure that somewhat resembled Woody Woodpecker spin around and release a stick of gum into a receiving tray. The machine didn't get a lot of use, and the gum was often a bit stale, but it was a good show.

An equally fascinating spectator sport was watching the little carriers that sped cash to and from the counters at the J.M. McDonald store. I never did quite figure out how those things worked. I only know that after one of the clerks, perhaps Eddie Johnson who later owned the store, placed a sales slip and cash payment into the little clip on the carrier, they pulled a cord and the thing whizzed to the back corner of the store where someone made change and sent the car speeding back on its wire rail. The clerk then unscrewed the little can, removed the change, and completed the transaction. I remember sitting on the benches near the entrance watching the little devices race back and forth on a busy Saturday night.

But, time and technology march on. Both of these marvels had to finally give way to a new attraction that demanded the attention of folks on Main Street. This exciting bit of wonder was perhaps as much as any single factor responsible for the disappearance of "Saturday Night in Town" as many of us knew it. It appeared in the window of Horbach's Gamble Store, where one could stop to watch a few moments of Herb Shriner or Omaha Wrestling on that new and wonderful device, a television set.

Five at a Time

Just one would have been enough to cause a stir. After all, even a little temptation is dangerous to impressionable minds. But five! Five caused flushed cheeks and could bring a thump to the heart. Five at a time could put a spring in the step and a tremble to the hand. Five at once! One hardly knew where to turn or which way to go first. The beauty! The allure! Those curves!

On a crisp, fall Saturday night, when the harvest moon was rich and full, the menfolk stepped out onto Manning's Main Street, raised their heads, took deep breaths, and inhaled the sweet aroma of ... New Cars! The new models had arrived at Manning's five auto dealerships.

They were all open for business. Up the hill to Ross for a look at the new Fords, down the hill and around the corner to Frahm Motor to see the Studebakers, then up Main Street for the ultimate thrill – three auto dealers on one corner: Fred Petersen's Dodge showroom, Struve's Buick/Jeep dealership, and Bock's Chevy garage.

That's right, Manning had five automobile dealerships. It seems impossible that a community of Manning's size could have supported five dealerships, but one must remember that back then the rural population was likely five times larger than today. Farmers drove cars and pickups, and many of the small businesses that served the farm families needed cars and trucks to carry out their services.

On Saturday night it was not uncommon to wind up parking a couple of blocks off Main Street because of all the cars. That was the era of five grocery stores, two drug stores, three hardware stores, four clothing stores, and two shoe stores – not to mention barber shops, shoe repair shops, a dry cleaners, three hardware stores, two furniture stores, two drug stores, three or four restaurants, and half a dozen taverns – all on Main Street It was a different time.

One fall evening each year, Main Street had a special attraction. The showrooms were a buzz with comments such as, "Cool, man!"...

"A hundred, at least."... "What in blazes do you want with four headlights?"... "All the extras: radio, heater, and overdrive."

Fairlanes, Bel Aires, Roadmasters, Coronets, and Presidents were the celebrities and we were their fans. There were ooh's and aah's over power steering, automatic transmissions, V-8 engines, and two- (or even three) tone paint jobs.

By 2005 standards, those machines were almost primitive. But in a time when more than a few '30s and '40s vintage autos still graced the road, those buggies were fresh and state of the art. The cars were all exciting, but a few stood apart from the rest. High school car buffs gazed longingly when "Putt Putt" Stahl cruised up Main in that sharp '55 Ford Fairlane. One either loved or hated the two-story tail fins on Dr. Drennen's DeSoto and when Henry Hoffman's '56 Studebaker Golden Hawk glided up the street with its huge Supercharged Packard V-8 purring through dual exhausts, all heads turned.

One suspects that there were a few tense moments along country roads late those Saturday nights, when starry-eyed husbands gave glowing accounts of those gleaming chariots and how affordable they really were to farm wives who were sewing aprons and school clothes out of flour sacks. But those five dealers sold cars. The sad irony of the situation is that those new, quiet, smooth running cars carried folks further and faster to bigger cities in search of better auto deals.

Saturday nights in October will never be the same.

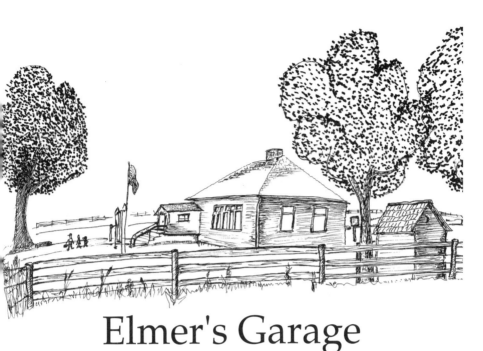

Elmer's Garage

In recent years it was Elmer Mueller's garage. Currently it's someone else's garage. For me and some others though, it's more than just an interesting old building. That building was Ewoldt No. 2, our school.

For generations that old one-room building stood on the northeast corner of the intersection two miles north and one mile east of Manning. (For real old-timers, Nellie Lynch's corner.) At that time it was one of a network of rural schools planted every two miles in each direction throughout the countryside. These schools were symbols of the dedication of rural Iowans to provide a quality education for their children.

The old school perhaps never knew an enrollment of more than 25 students in one year, but it seemed like an enormous place to me as a child. When I think of the events - like the Christmas program when a wire, stretched across the room, held bed sheets for a stage curtain and white gas mantle lamps hung from ceiling hooks providing light, and all the school families gathered to watch students perform - the memory assumes Carnegie Hall proportion. Now when I pause on the sidewalk during each return visit to Manning, the old building seems just too small.

During the Manning Centennial a high school reunion was held. It was enjoyable to bask in the noise of happy greetings and cries of remembrance, but for me there was another, quieter reunion. Walking around Elmer's garage one morning I could almost see and hear Gary and Linda Handlos, Stan and Ken Spies, Ruth, Laurel, and Cleo Singsank, Larry and Darlene Genzen, Betty Lengemann and all the others with whom I shared that room. I could hear Golda Sander, Loretta Lerssen, and Irma Bromert as they taught. I remembered when some older boys decided that the furnace was the appropriate disposal place for a pile of sweeping compound causing the immediate evacuation of the building. I saw the coat hooks hung with snow-wet clothes and the crockery water cooler in the little hallway, and the basement drain that backed up in wet weather. I could smell the oiled floor and the coal furnace. I saw Jack Mohr and Glenn Singsank's carved initials still visible in the siding above the place where the storm cellar once lay.

I certainly don't suggest a mass pilgrimage across the current owner's lawn to view the old schoolhouse, but in the words of a former Carroll merchant, "If you can't stop, smile as you go by." Ask a former rural school student or a former teacher about rural school education. Ask them about outhouses in January or movies in the high school gym with the County Superintendent, or eighth grade graduation in Carroll.

Rural schools had their limitations, but we got a good education, and we farm boys would rather have stood by the schoolyard fence watching Alfred Ahrendsen plow with his new John Deere tractor than play dodge ball during recess anyway.

A Scentimental Journey

Did you ever wish you could be transported back in time; not permanently, mind you, but just for a little while? Have you ever wondered what it would be like to experience just one little part of life from years back while keeping your present age, knowledge, and view of life? I think that sometimes it might be very interesting.

For instance, I'd like to spend about one hour in my rural school right after Noon recess on a cold, snowy winter day.

Picture it. Fifteen or so elementary and junior high-aged kids had just come in from recess. Having been outside running around in the snow, we were all kind of sweaty inside those warm coats and snow suits. Since our mittens, gloves, scarves, and snow pants (Remember those, ladies?) were wet, we placed them on the floor furnace register to dry. Many of the farms did not have indoor bathtubs or showers, so many of the farm kids got one good bath each week on Saturday night with hand and face washings filling the gaps. The shoes and overshoes worn by especially the older boys had perhaps seen double duty that day for both school and helping with the morning chores. It may be that just the faintest trace of something unpleasant clung to the treads of overshoes or around the sole of a shoe. A little moisture from melted snow brought it all to life. All of this activity takes place in a single room about the size of a two-car garage.

Nope, I would not be as interested in the sights and sounds as – *The Smells!* My guess is that we were a pretty aromatic bunch. I recall the smell of drying mittens and all that, but it didn't seem to make much of an impression then. It probably all seemed fairly normal. However, it had to bear some resemblance to the evenings that I transported my son and two large friends home each night from junior high football practice in my little Datsun station wagon. "I don't care how cold it is, the windows stay open!"

Maybe that's why Mrs. Sander and Mrs. Bromert always insisted that fresh air from an open window was good for us, even in the winter.

I read somewhere that the deodorant industry was a prime example of 20th century marketing: you create a need, convince people of that need, and then market a product to fill the need. We are daily being sent the message that personal odor is a grave social offense. Basketball star Charles Barkley pitched underarm deodorant as a necessary social grace, while riding a horse to a fox hunt. One deodorant company hints that body odor must be avoided even while doing one's workout at a gym. (What would you do if the babe or hunk at the next weight set caught a whiff of perspiration? It could be disastrous!)

I acknowledge that many of these commercials are tongue-in-cheek. However, our society's attitude toward, and tolerance of, odors has definitely changed over the years. Certainly, our vision of personal cleanliness has changed as well.

Health textbooks of the early and mid-century hinted that daily baths were unnecessary and perhaps unhealthy and drying to one's skin. Hair washing was recommended on a once-every-two-week schedule so as to maintain cleanliness and yet avoid removing necessary and lustrous natural oils. As a matter of fact, I'm not sure what many of us from the "duck tail" generation would have done without a several day residue of Vaseline Hair Tonic and Butch Wax to keep those sculptured hairdos in place. Shoot, we could walk from the bus to MHS in a 40-mile-an-hour gale, and our locks wouldn't even twitch. Lest you get too smug girls, remember those beehive hairdos of the '60s. You'd have died without that heavy-duty hair spray. You could have stiffened rope into fence posts with that stuff.

All silliness aside, it would be fun to take a magic trip back to a certain moment in time just to see what it was like. There would probably be lots of noticeable little social differences just like the odor issue. What seems perfectly normal in one generation seems perfectly weird in another. Have you thrown away your bell bottoms, your poodle skirt, or your penny loafers?

Or ... perhaps such trips back in time wouldn't be as interesting as they seem. Maybe a *half* hour in the country school after Noon recess would be sufficient.

From The Heart

Every year about this time, someone with too much time on their hands adds up what all the gifts mentioned in the song "Twelve Days of Christmas" would cost at current prices. Whenever and wherever that bit of not-very-useful information appears, conversations usually move in the direction of "Things sure cost a lot more than they used to." It's tempting and a little bit depressing to recount what prices were listed on various gift items 10, 20 or more years ago.

Christmas gift giving does seem to be more expensive than it used to be. The price tags on dolls, clothing, bicycles, and other traditional gifts can produce some real shivers in the pocketbook. In addition, modern advertising points us in the direction of a "more is better" ethic of giving, and it is hinted that the more elaborate and expensive a gift is, the more love and care is shown by the giver and the more it is appreciated by the recipient.

That philosophy of giving is certainly open to debate. There are many gifts that, while not expensive in a financial sense, convey love far beyond their dollar value.

In the midst of all our expensive gifts and decorations they are found. They're not made of gold, silver, or other precious metals. More likely they're made of jar rings, cardboard, plywood, cotton, and shellac. They were not handcrafted in quaint European workshops or precision factories. Rather, they were glued, stapled, or taped together in very non-quaint and imprecise workshops. Not the products of highly skilled hands and years of apprenticeship, they were simply labors of love, crafted by hands more used to other, less artistic pursuits.

In the salesman-like view of the advertiser, these unrefined artifacts do not deserve the places of honor they occupy nor do they deserve to be among the more exquisite decorations that surround them. But that critical view has a major blind spot; it doesn't see the love that went into the making and giving of these handmade treasures. A craft item by a close friend carries as many good wishes as far more expensive do-dads, and the handmade gifts from school children to parents – ah, gold itself couldn't hold such value.

What home does not display plaster cast handprints, cotton and cardboard tree ornaments, jar ring picture frames, or various other such items? Slightly rumpled matchbox manger scenes, crooked Styrofoam snowmen, and bread dough teddy bears annually take the place of honor they have held since proud hands presented them to smiling parents years ago. Expensive? Hardly. Valuable? Absolutely!

Golda Sander, teacher of Ewoldt No. 2, was a really ambitious gift planner; or perhaps she was simply determined to give that bunch of boys something to do with their hands besides poke one another and draw pictures. In either case, our rural school had an "industrial arts" shop. It was a cold little room in the school basement where coping saws coped, planes planed, hammers hammered, and products were produced. By means of much encouragement and some patterns brought from somewhere, Mrs. Sander supervised the construction of waving Santa Claus cutouts, sleigh and reindeer sets, and whole flocks of hen and chicken lawn silhouettes.

After much sawing, hammering, and painting, these wonderful gifts were wrapped and presented to proud and understanding parents at the school Christmas program. Perhaps it was the dim light from the single bulb light fixtures that caused smiling fathers not to notice the thumbprints in Santa's beard or mothers to overlook the fact that Donner had only one antler. They were always surprised (How do you wrap an 18-inch Masonite lawn chicken so that it doesn't look like an 18-inch Masonite lawn chicken?) and never disappointed.

That was just one little school on one little country corner, but the story is the same from country to city. We've spent a lot of money on Christmas gifts over the years, and we'll probably spend a lot more; but none of that fancy stuff will ever mean more than one painted plate with Santa, five green reindeer, and the words, Merry Christmas, Mom and Dad.

Food of Memory

The very sight of the supermarket cooler item brought this aging farm boy to a dead stop. It was the last thing I ever expected to see in this city store. Clean, skinned, neatly wrapped, and ready to be taken home - the stacks of chicken feet drew curious glances from adults and exclamations of delight from children.

My mind skipped back to boyhood, when occasionally, for a novelty, my mother would make a pot of chicken foot soup. It was always a mystery that anything as bony and unappealing as chicken feet could be made into anything useful, much less a meal that people would actually eat. But, sure enough, when that leathery, yellow skin was removed there was indeed enough delicate white meat to make a very acceptable chicken soup.

But, that was a long time ago! Who could possibly want to buy chicken feet or make chicken foot soup in this day and age?

Simple...the same people who ate chicken foot soup back then. People who had lived in another culture, perhaps in dire poverty, and came with what they could carry in their hands to a new land where they too might have a chance at a full and free life. Oh, the names are different. Instead of Musfeldt, Schmidt, or Rowedder they are called Nguyen, Tranh, or Alvarez. The idea, however, is the same: come to this new land of opportunity and bring along the old ways and values. One of the most important of those poverty-born values: don't waste anything!

An Italian immigrant friend told me the story of how pizza came into being. "We didn't have all the meat in the old country that we have here. We had maybe one chicken a week for the whole family. We had to do everything to make it stretch. So, we made meat sauces from tomatoes and spices and put it on a flat cake of bread with some cheese. We all had plenty to eat and it tasted good. Now people think it's a delicacy. For my parents it was a way to feed the family." My friend also told me that for a real treat they substituted squash blossoms for slices of tomato as a pizza topping.

Don't waste anything! In our current "buy too much, use what you want, and throw the rest away" culture, that mentality seems old-fashioned and kind of quaint. Americans have lived in a land of plenty for so long that we've forgotten what it meant to our ancestors to simply have enough to eat.

The immigrant families that buy and eat chicken feet, hog snouts, and fish heads remember all too well. Some of them have managed to get a toe hold on the American dream and can afford more expensive foods, but they still come back to that meat counter. The foods of poverty have become foods of tradition. Those chicken feet are their version of our German-American head cheese, grit voos, and blood sausage. They are culturally traditional, seen by many as delicacies, perhaps viewed in disgust by others, and rich with memories. They are foods made from those things which the wealthy can afford to throw away, that which goes to waste.

Maybe my mother was teaching us more than how to make soup out of something unexpected. Maybe that was a valuable reminder of where we came from and how richly we are blessed. And maybe it was a unique and delicious way of underlining an important lesson – **Don't Waste Anything!**

The Men Wore Hats and The Women Wore Dresses

One of my favorite pictures in the Manning Centennial Book, *We Can Remember* is found on page 88 – a mid-'50s Children's Day parade. Talk about Manning in a nutshell. There's almost too much to see in that one picture: the old fire station and library building still standing, the Willys Jeep sign hanging on the side of the Struve Motor building, the whole row of businesses where the Plaza now stands, a sunny June day at noon (note the shadows are straight down), an old model pickup parked on the corner by the Klean Klose Shop, all the women wearing dresses and the men wearing straw hats.

In that picture, the parade spectators and participants were heavily balanced toward women. That was the height of the farm-family era around Manning. Most of the men and quite a few of the boys were home working on the farms. On such a sunny June day there may have been hay to make or corn to be cultivated.

Perhaps on many farms there had been a slightly early dinner or dishes washed faster than usual to allow farm wives to hurriedly change and get the kids to town in time for the Children's Day parade. Many came later in the day.

There was only one parade leader in Manning in those days - Harry Koester, riding that high-stepping palomino. Falling into positions behind Harry were fire trucks, the high school and junior high bands in uniform, and hundreds of children. It has been said that some of those parades numbered more than 1,000 participants. That's more than half the population of the town in those days. Many of the now empty farm places around the countryside were occupied by families then. It seemed that everyone in the country came to Children's Day.

In fact, that was the question of the hour on the lips of many in the days before. My grandparents would ask if we were going to "Kinderball." Between the kids, it was simply, "Are you going to Children's Day?"

The parade concluded at the Fireman's Hall, transformed for the day into a bustling amusement park. There was a large concession stand, a rifle shooting contest for the boys and softball throwing contest for the girls, a merry-go-round, a Ferris wheel, a kiddie car ride, a dunking tank, and tons of children. And that's how the afternoon went. Take your turn shooting or throwing, walk around with friends, buy a popsicle, walk around with friends, watch some other kids shoot or throw, walk around with friends, get in a water pistol fight, walk around with friends, go on one of the rides, walk around with friends, and as we got older, check out the prospects for the main event - the evening dance.

For those of us from the country, supper time meant a break in the action. Many of us were lucky enough to have relatives in town where we could go for a meal somewhat healthier than we'd been eating all afternoon. Grandpa and Grandma Musfeldt or Uncle Albert and Aunt Arlene were gracious enough to let me and my brother and sister invade their homes for a "time out." We got a chance to sit down, rest, eat, wash up, and change clothes. I have some fond memories of those evenings.

And then, back to the action.

Pete Kuhl, Gary Schroeder, George Fischer, Ralph Grundmeier, and Bonita Hagedorn were warmed up and ready to play! The spotlights sent sparkling stars of light dancing off the big mirrored ball hanging from the ceiling. While mothers in dresses and fathers in straw hats watched from the sidelines, shy glances and timid steps became more confident as the King and Queen for the day led off the first dance. No matter if the songs being played were ever so slightly out of date, little children danced and adults smiled. When the band broke into its own version of the Bunny Hop, the wooden dance floor creaked and bounced. Could the old place handle the strain? It was reported that in Des Moines the floor in one dance hall collapsed from the Bunny Hop.

When the little kids began to tire and get cranky, families would pack up and head for home. The dance floor would thin down to the older kids, and certain couples seemed to dance more exclusively with one another. Some took a break for a moonlight ride on the Ferris wheel or a bottle of pop.

One quick stop at the concession stand on the way to the car was like a ritual. They sold little rubber balls attached to a long rubber string - sort of a rubber ball yo-yo. Depending on how much of the hard-earned and long-saved money remained, I always bought a "nickel ball" or a "dime ball." In the days following, a few bounces could bring back just a bit of the fun and magic of that day meant just for us kids.

Keep Your Eyes on the Sky

It's really amazing - the technology they use. It seems like every few months one of them gets a new computer, or a fancier set of maps, or someone comes up with some new scientific explanation for the same old stuff - all this just to predict the weather.

Every television weatherman (or woman) has their own gimmick from satellite photos of weather fronts to cute little computer graphic storm clouds with flickering lightening bolts.

From Willard Scott on down, these Wizards of Weather go by fancy names like "Head Meteorologist" and get paid big bucks to tell us whether or not it's going to rain tomorrow. Some cities have "Weather Services" which, for a fee, draw up elaborate forecast charts with lots of numbers and lines at the request of area farmers and other companies whose work schedules are greatly affected by the weather.

And we all spend time sitting and watching them!

Now, this is not all that new. We've always been interested in the weather. Farmers have traditionally had a vested interest in the weather as they prepared to cut hay, plant corn, or combine oats, but they didn't get so technical about it. They'd just tune the radio to an Omaha station and if it was raining in Nebraska today, it was a fairly good bet that it would rain in Iowa tomorrow.

However good the forecasters thought they were in those days, lots of folks - city and country - had as much faith in another system. They looked at the sky. No, this is not one of those "Look up and if your face gets wet, expect rain" gags. Folks used to watch the moon.

Remember how most calendars showed full moon and new moon dates? A quick glance shows that the calendar on our kitchen wall gives the usual dates, holidays, and the full moon dates. Another one down the hall gives not only the full moon, but new moon, first quarter, and last quarter dates. Occasionally one can still see a calendar with little fish symbols indicating which days they'll likely be biting. Since those calendars are probably printed a year or so in advance in Chicago or some such place, what the dickens do they know about the bullheads in Black Hawk Lake in June? It's all in the moon.

People have historically looked at the moon for clues to weather and nature. In generations past, certain stages of the moon were considered to be important in deciding planting and harvesting dates. Indeed, Frank Field, that long-time weatherman at KMA, Shenandoah, regularly gave the moon sign dates with the daily forecast, and many folks believed that the moon sign dates were the more important of the two items. I remember hearing my grandparents insisting that potatoes planted at the right moon sign were definitely going to do better than if planted on another day.

With regard to weather forecasting, certain other lunar events were significant. The weather on the day of a moon change was said to predict the weather for the next two weeks. A ring around the moon was a sign of approaching rain. The number of stars visible inside the ring predicted the number of days it would rain.

An unusual heavenly sight, called "sun dogs" occurring in winter was said to predict severe cold. Those bright lights flanking the sun were a sign to bundle up and light the stove.

Another weather predictor had to do with the religious calendar. Certain days called Ember Days were also said to predict the weather.

Sound like hocus-pocus or old wives' tales? Well, maybe. But, since all such things are based in some fact, however obscure, it might be interesting to do some scientific studies, comparing the television forecast with the predictions of someone's grandmother or grandfather and see who's more accurate.

Real scientific people will scoff and say that all that moon stuff is just superstition from an older and less sophisticated age. However, since most calendars still show moon sign dates or at least full and last quarter moon, it looks like a good bit of modern society is still looking at the sky.

Forecast: Cold!
Part I

Sometime during the course of a Midwest winter came that dreaded one word weather forecast: COLD! Oh, weathermen coined fancy phrases to dress it up: "Frigid Arctic Blast" or "Siberia Express." However, one word said it all: COLD! Not just "cold" when the car windshields had to be scraped free of morning frost or the pumpkins and squash were brought in for safekeeping; not just "cold" when you had to lower your ear flaps or put on gloves, but COLD!

This forecast was for COLD weather when tree limbs cracked and creaked on the stillest morning, when the thermometer showed 20, 25, or even 30 degrees below zero, when wagon boxes and barn doors cracked like a gunshot when they were bumped.

This forecast was for COLD weather when the barn cats' milk pan was frozen solid with the remains of last evening's meal, when the pail of luke-warm water brought from the house to wash the cows' udders before milking steamed like a boiler in this, the warmest area outside the farm house itself.

This forecast was for COLD weather when children in town got a ride to school because the walk of only a few blocks risked actual frostbite of fingers, toes, and earlobes that peeked out from under stocking caps.

Fifty or more years ago COLD meant scary times for Iowans. COLD was the weather condition that spelled immediate and serious problems for any home that lost its heat source. Homes were heated by coal, wood, or oil burning stoves and furnaces that blazed furiously to battle the monster outside. More than one house caught fire when something went wrong at such a time, and many of us from that era might have slept less soundly had we known how close the old, dry lumber around superheated chimneys and stovepipes came to bursting spontaneously into flames.

When COLD was accompanied by wind the problems intensified. The old farm houses and many city houses just couldn't hold out those frigid blasts that rattled windows and penetrated any crack in siding or around foundations. It wasn't uncommon to see houses with a tar paper air seal around the foundation or, in the country, a row of hay or straw bales fitted around the outside of the foundation as an insulating fortress against the biting COLD wind.

COLD wasn't just annoying or inconvenient; it was painful, brutal, and dangerous to people, wildlife, and farm livestock. It posed some peculiar problems that had to be solved…stay tuned.

Forecast: Cold!
Part II

I don't remember exactly when it became my job, but sometime during my early teens, Dad showed me how to light the heating lamps in the livestock waterers.

It seems like a peculiar problem to have in the midst of all that ice and snow, but when it got COLD, water shortages became a problem for farmers. Not exactly the same as in summer when wells got low or lack of wind kept windmills from pumping water from well to cistern or water tank, but a water shortage problem nonetheless. The main problem: water freezes into ice, and thirsty animals and people can't drink ice. Moreover, when it's COLD, water will freeze in pipes deep underground and ice doesn't flow through faucets and hydrants. Now that's a crisis!

The forecast is COLD! With long term preparations made, such as pipelines buried deeply and windmill and hydrant boxes covered with two-foot-deep layers of insulating livestock manure (...sound odd? Ask an old farmer.), attention was turned to the watering units themselves. Even today, the odor of burning kerosene brings to mind the image of trudging through crusty snow with the five-gallon can of kerosene in one hand and the scissors and matches in the pocket of my gray coveralls. Every evening the cover plates were opened to expose the kerosene lamps located in the small compartment under the waterer. Depending on the size of the waterer, one, two, or even three metal tanks were filled with kerosene, wicks were trimmed, and lamps were lighted. The lamp burners produced enough heat to keep the water from freezing in even the coldest weather.

In the henhouse, where cooped-up chickens would peck at the frost crystals forming on the inside of the walls, the kerosene lamps served a dual purpose. In addition to keeping the chicken waterers from freezing solid even inside the building, the lamps gave off just enough heat to temper the icy weather outside and keep frostbitten chicken combs to a minimum.

Sometimes, too much water was a problem. Farmers would rig windmills to turn at a very slow speed and let them run constantly to keep a slow flow of water moving in the pipes between well and farm place cistern, simply to prevent pipeline freezing. A windmill pumping too long into an overfilled reservoir would produce a big sheet of ice on the farmyard. The COLD does its work quickly.

One particular day, the wind had been blowing all day. The heavy snowfall began about noon. Right before supper Dad said, "Shoot, the windmill is still going. With this wind we'll have ice all over the yard by morning. Grab a flashlight and run down quick and turn it off." (Or words to that effect.)

The flashlight penetrated only a few feet into the blowing snow, and the accumulated two feet or so of dry, white powder on top of residue from previous snowfalls made "running down quick" a slow process. I didn't feel any particular sense of danger. After all, the windmill was only a few hundred yards away, and the trip had been made scores of times. But, why didn't Dad think of this earlier?

The dry creek was not even in my mind until the ground suddenly dropped out from under my feet, the flashlight flew, and I was kind of floating in a lake of snow with my outspread arms providing support and my feet a few inches off the creek bed. No real sense of danger yet; just irritation with my father, that lousy windmill, and the whole situation. At this point I realized that, with nowhere to brace my feet, I couldn't climb out. Remembering having read something somewhere about this kind of predicament, I lay over to one side and sort of rolled along, spreading my weight over the surface of the shifting snow. Out! I'll have to remember to cross at a different spot on the way back. Just turn off the stupid windmill and get home where it's warm.

I found the windmill, little thanks to the dim light of my ice covered flashlight. Turning away from the shut-down windmill, I discovered two things: first, the falling snow was so thick I couldn't see the lights of the farm place at all. Second, within only a few yards, the wind had blown my tracks closed and I had no trail home. A slight shiver of danger began to prod my creativity.

Locating the fence line that I knew was not far to my left, I followed the barbed wire toward the farm place until the glow of our yard light came into view. It was a more welcoming sight than usual.

Only later that evening did I begin to fully realize the potential danger of that snowy trip. Then I got kind of scared.

You don't mess around and get careless when it's COLD!

The Rites of Spring

It happens every year. One lovely spring morning, the sun begins to warm the soil with its newly discovered strength, the birds serenade the coming season, the fragile greenery of buds and grass venture into a new world, and this transplanted farm boy gets the insane urge to go out and plow something.

Ah, spring on the farm! How I long to be back home in the open air feeling the slightly cutting wind in my face as the big tractor purrs along drawing the plow..., no, the first spring task was disking corn stalk ground for oats seeding.

Ah, spring! The beginnings of new life all around, the disk cutting through last season's cornstalks releasing a pungent fragrance...hold it...ah, yes, *now* I remember the *first* spring task.

Ah, phooey! I don't miss one bit that first spring excursion into the still soggy fields dragging that clattering, smelly machine around.

Former farm kids are way ahead of me by now. There was nothing noble, romantic or glamorous about the first task of spring. When a farmer feeds livestock all winter in enclosed barns and sheds, the inevitable result is...manure.

There is no real delicate way of saying it. The stuff is there, and it needs to be hauled away. Whether you scooped it with a shovel, loaded it with a loader, or pitched it with a fork, the end result was the same. Before you disked or plowed all that fragrant Iowa soil there was the matter of distributing something decidedly more fragrant to disk or plow *under* that fragrant Iowa soil.

It wasn't something just anyone could do; there was some skill involved. One had to know how thick to spread which variety on what type of soil. There was some meteorological knowledge required; it was important to discern which way the wind was blowing before starting the unloading phase of the operation. Depth perception came in handy. Without it, one could spend quite some time straightening the teeth on a manure loader after trying to lift one end of the barn along with the material at hand. Finally, there was the muscle development phase which began after one had done as much as possible with modern machinery, and the corners and edges were still untouched.

Well, perhaps it wasn't as big a deal as all that. But it was not the kind of job a high school boy wanted to do for an hour before school in the morning, not if he wanted any friends. It was a dirty job, and someone had to do it; but why me?

Before writing this little chapter, I wrestled with the problem of how to delicately deal with the subject. Apparently other writers have encountered this too. I got a chuckle out of a recent Perry Mason television rerun from back in the days when television dialog was more polite. Perry Mason was asked to defend a young girl accused of killing a stable hand with something called a "spreader." My puzzlement was solved in the courtroom scene when the prosecutor displayed Exhibit A, the murder weapon—a four tine manure fork.

It's Polka Time

Had the Midwest adopted a national (or regional) anthem during the 1940s or '50s, it might well have been a polka. Many Midwestern folks were emigrants from Germany, Czechoslovakia or Scandinavia. Local communities still retained strong cultural ties with nations of origin. Even the names of towns such as Westphalia or Holstein were taken directly from European countries. Cultural ties to land of origin included musical tastes. Local radio stations had their "Polka Time" programs, and while city radio stations such as WHO in Des Moines entertained its listeners with Bill Austin on the piano and KIOA served up a steady diet of Buddy Holly and Bill Haley to the budding rock and roll generation, WNAX in Yankton, South Dakota, and the newly started KCIM in Carroll featured Whoopee John, the Six Fat Dutchmen, and Johnny Matuska and the Bohemian Band.

For many Midwest homes, the sounds of polkas, waltzes, and schottisches provided the background music at mealtime. In my own memory, hot summer days, dinner in our farm kitchen and polkas on KCIM are woven inseparably into a single fabric.

In a way, the polka, or German dance music in general, was the common denominator of that era. Parents who detested that "racket" from pop stations and teenagers who moaned at the very mention of Guy Lombardo both happily danced polkas and schottisches. Whether at Children's Day with Pete Kuhl or at the Starline in Carroll with the Six Fat Dutchmen, there was a common core of tunes that were enjoyed and danced to by all ages.

People still dance to German music. The Polka Lovers Klub of America promotes polka bands and events around the country. Weihnachtsfest-style German festivals in various states celebrate the German-American heritage, but it's not quite the same. Being one more generation removed from our immigrant roots does make a difference. Television, stereo, and the Internet have surely widened our horizons. We can tailor our personal environment to our own tastes as never before, but perhaps we've lost a little something in the process: a daily sense of common history and heritage.

It would be a bit surprising to see a Whoopee John tune on the Top 40 of 2006, but these days people could benefit by finding a common thread that could pull them together and provide a common means of celebration.

A-one-and-a-two-and…I guess you had to be there.

The Longest Day of School

With the possible exception of the last day of spring, this was the longest day of the school year. It really didn't matter what the weather was like, although a crisp, sunny, autumn day would make matters even worse. We boys had been waiting for weeks for this day to dawn and now that it was here, the sweet agony was almost unbearable.

Irma Bromert could have jumped through hoops or swallowed fire, and she still wouldn't have been able to hold our attention for long. Arithmetic seemed even less relevant than usual as the hands on the wall clock crept slowly toward high noon. Anxious eyes had trouble focusing on the addition problems in the arithmetic drill book, and tense fingers just couldn't seem to coax the pencil into making numbers when there was something so much more significant to do.

The hands met at the top of the schoolhouse clock. Now dismissed, we grabbed our lunch pails and walked as fast as we dared out the front door of the school building. None of us wanted to be halted for running in the building and be made to go back and walk out slowly; time was precious. Breaking into a full sprint, we dashed to the edge of the road bank where there was an unobstructed view of the Great Western railroad tracks running through Alvan Hansen's pasture. With any luck we were able to get settled into a good spot before the action began.

At barely minutes after noon the first volley echoed up and down the Nishnabotna River bottom – pheasant season had officially opened. The hunters, lucky grownups who didn't have anything else to do, who had sat on auto fenders at the railroad crossing waiting for the Manning noon whistle to sound, now began their march through the horseweed, bootjack, and wild rose thickets along the tracks. With a mixture of envy and irritation ("Those guys will shoot them all before we're home from school! Why can't we get out at noon?"), we watched and listened as the cackle of rooster pheasants and "pop" of shotgun reports punctuated our lunchtime conversation. No sounds for a while. "Ha! Those ring necks are way too smart for those town hunters. We know where to look." "Did you clean your gun last night? I'm going to use number six shot." "Real hunters don't need dogs; they just get in the way." "I wish I had a 12-gauge; my .410 just isn't big enough."

And that's the way it was on Veterans Day in the early 1950s - the rites of fall, and growing up, and being privileged to live in a place that offered such exotic pastimes as pheasant hunting. It was the thrill of the chase, the excitement of that burst of golden wings that put a boy into momentary shock, the pounding of the heart, the sense of adventure, of really being alive and tuned in to every sight and sound of a fall day – and occasionally even bagging a pheasant.

What Did You Say?

Having developed the sometimes embarrassing habit of talking to myself, it wasn't unusual for me to close my desk, push back the chair and make some audible comment about the day's trials and tribulations. This day, however, a new twist was added: I couldn't believe what I'd said.

>Me: What did you just say?
>Myself: I said, "Time to go to hoos."
>Me: What in the world does **that** mean?
>Myself: If I remember right, it was a line I heard Dad say when I was a kid – it means "Time to go home." It's sort of a mixture of English and German. It happened all the time.
>Me: What on earth made you come up with that after all these years?
>Myself: Second childhood? Wow! I really don't know...kind of spooky, isn't it? I must have heard it a hundred times back then...

Manning didn't celebrate Weihnachtsfest in those days, and Children's Day had few German overtones (even though some of the older people referred to it as "Kinderball"), but German culture was as close as that little curb on the front of Hank Peters' tavern. That was the place where older men gathered to smoke and visit. They talked about every imaginable topic ranging from family and farming to weather and worries. They visited for hours—mostly in German.

Many of those men were immigrants who had come as children from Schleswig-Holstein, Germany, to America around the turn of the century. Some were American born children of immigrant parents. Most were not consciously trying to preserve German culture, but they all spoke German.

Their wives spoke German while shopping or socializing. On Sunday mornings at Zion Lutheran Church, Pastor John Ansorge would preach one German service for the benefit of these folks. Many of their children had received their catechism instruction "Auf Deutsch." All the store clerks spoke English, but to do business in Manning, it didn't hurt to speak some German.

People's names were even different. A neighbor, Henry J. M. Hansen, was often called Heinie.

Mom, why do they call him Heinie?
It's short for Heinrich.
Well, that really clears that up – I thought his name was Henry.
Heinrich is German for Henry.
Oh.

Say Kuhl for me. In much of the country it rhymes with cool. All Oregon Schroeders are Shrow (rhymes with throw) ders. And you wouldn't believe the trouble I have with Musfeldt!

Last name please...... Was that Mansfeld?... Newfelt?... Roosevelt?... (Sigh) M-U-S-F (as in Frank)-E-L-D-T.

The children of immigrants kept a fair amount of their parents' language. Into the '50s and '60s German phrases and words were still used in conversations. Parents often used Plattdeutsch to keep certain information from the ears of their children. Main Street conversations were still often bilingual.

My generation has totally lost the old tongue – or so I'd thought. Then came that "hoos" episode. The roots indeed go deep. Whether we know it or not, my generation is still part of that German heritage. We are the children of those people who came to this country in search of better lives for themselves and their families. To this new land they brought their culture and their language. Both have changed with time, but both still exist. That's good. It gives us a sense of past, present, and future.

Some folks in our part of the U.S. are very worried and irritated because of all the Latin American immigrants who insist on speaking Spanish to one another. I just say, Relax. Give 'em two or three generations and they'll be talking to themselves, just like the rest of us.

In Good Hands

In my role as a professional church worker, I was periodically called upon to assist the pastor in serving communion. It was on Ash Wednesday as I placed the wafers of bread in the outstretched hands of our parishioners, that I noticed the difference. The difference was so great that I was momentarily distracted from the task at hand and was transported back to other communions and other altars of long ago.

At the communion rail there were elderly hands and youthful hands. There were feminine and masculine hands. Most were the hands of people who work at gentle professions: clerical workers, computer operators, businessmen. We moved down the tables of devout worshippers, touching their hands with the symbols of their faith.

Then I came to Steve's hands. His hands were not soft and smooth. They were not used to gentle tasks, but rough. These hands did not earn their bread easily. They were the hands of a farmer. Steve, his father, and his brother farm some 1,500 acres of Willamette valley soil. They grow crops quite different from most of those around Manning. But the results of that farm labor were the same as those around Manning...calluses.

I don't get many calluses these days, and so the sight of that farmer's hands caught my eye and jogged my memory. I remember when *my* hands were like that, when no amount of scrubbing or rubbing with any kind of hand cream could erase the prints of farming.

My father's hands were the same. So were those of our neighbors - the Eischeids, the Hagedorns, Sonksens, and Schrums, the Bruhns, Hansens, Muhlbauers, Rohes, and all the rest. There were no exceptions. In those days especially, we earned our living with our hands.

And it wasn't just the men. Wives, too, lived with a far different standard of smoothness than today's urban folk. Often wives worked side by side with their husbands, marking feminine hands with the badge of rural living ...calluses.

Our hands were well acquainted with the business end of a No. 12 aluminum shovel. Many of us didn't have small, portable augers to move grain. We shoveled it. We shoveled corn into a grinder, oats into a small granary, ground corn cobs into the laying barn, and soiled chicken litter out. In the summer we shoveled grain, and in the winter, snow. Shovels actually wore out.

We knew the shape of a fork handle ...oats bundles into the rack (pitch fork), out of the rack into the threshing machine, straw into a stack or baler (straw fork), hay into a hayrack or the manger, cattle manure (manure fork) into a spreader...the fork handle was no stranger.

Hands gripped corn knives for cutting button weeds or horseweeds, hoes for cutting cockleburs, wrenches for tightening cultivator shovels, hammers for repairing buildings, pliers for fixing fence, ropes for restraining livestock, wire or twine for throwing bales, and sledgehammers for splitting firewood.

Hands used to hard labor still needed to be gentle enough to hold a baby calf. They needed to be precise enough to make tiny adjustments on engines. They needed to be available for helping get a child ready for church on Sunday.

I suspect the teachers in school and the other students could also see from our hands that we were farm kids. There was no hiding one's hands in typing class. No potential girlfriend could mistake the fact that her suitor was a farm boy after the first, tentative touch of hands. We could put on a clean shirt, a sport coat, and shiny shoes, but we brought our callused hands to the school dance.

The process was quick. We would grasp the tool with determination and lean into the task. Soon came the twinge, "Rats! A blister." Then, in time, the callus. Hay baling, another callus. Walking corn rows, more calluses.

It could be worse. One slip while fixing fence and the barbed wire did more than make calluses. So would the shiny edge of a cultivator shovel, the slip of a Crescent wrench, the side of a loading chute, or two-cylinder John Deere tractors with the bright idea of putting the tool box right below the exhaust pipe.

No more. Now *my* hands are more used to the feel of power steering, the computer keypad, or the neck of a guitar. But back then...

I couldn't do it now. My hands are too soft.

But Steve's hands...they still can and do. So too, I imagine, can the hands of Kusels, Kienasts, Musfeldts, Mohrs, and all the others who still earn their living on the farm...with their hands.

Out the Kitchen Window

She saw life framed in her kitchen window. All good kitchens had windows, and the kitchen was her workshop. Oh, she would work in the yard or garden and help her husband with chores, but the kitchen was truly her domain.

The kitchen was the scene of early morning breakfasts, big dinners, and late suppers during the crop growing season. There, bread was kneaded and baked. There, garden vegetables were canned, as well as fruit brought home in lugs from the grocery store.

Through the kitchen window she saw the first robins of spring preening in the still leafless trees. The bubbling song of a house wren provided musical accompaniment to the rattle of breakfast dishes being washed. In the pasture she could see the milk cows walking single file toward their favorite grazing spot.

Hot summer weather and a wood and coal range combined to make the kitchen nearly unbearable. Cooking was done as early as possible on those days. Some farms still had separate summer kitchens.

The summer kitchen was hot too, but at least the whole house didn't get heated through.

She would pause in the midst of meal preparation to watch the angry gray-green clouds boil over the horizon. Through the window she saw her husband walking slowly toward the house, his shoulders a little less than square. The wind and hail had been efficient in their attack on the young crops.

On better days, she could hear the sound of his chore-time whistling float through the open window as the blue bottle flies buzzed and bounced against the screen.

The window was a frame for the picture of their children at play outside the farm house. It was a perfect place to look out for their safety and yet not let them see she was watching.

The fall leaves drifting past the window signaled the end of another growing season. At dusk, the gleam of the headlights on the corn picker flashed across the glass, and she would breathe a prayer of thanks for a safe harvest day on that dangerous machine.

Through the window she watched the children coming home from school on a fall afternoon. Later, she watched them drive away to college or the service and rejoiced to see their new families returning for a visit.

The old window rattled and shook in the sharp-edged wind. They had seen the pheasants moving into the grove the night before, and the morning light revealed dozens of the big birds perched high in the trees. A storm was headed this way. Soon the world through the window would be cold and white, and the kitchen would be a cozy haven from the winter's hardships.

The seasons of the year and the seasons of life—all framed, focused and viewed.

Whether it was a farm house or a house in town, they had one thing in common. Through the years, mothers have loved, watched over, and cared for their families through that viewpoint of life – the kitchen window.

Our Cottage Industry

Some time ago an article was published in a national magazine regarding the current methods of producing beef cattle in huge corporation-operated feedlots. The author of the article wrote that in the past, beef cattle production, especially in the Midwest, had been almost a "cottage industry." Upon first reading, the line sort of made me mad. The term "cottage industry" sounded quaint and condescending – almost insulting. The family farms of Iowa that produced some of the tastiest beef ever to grace the tables of big city magazine writers hardly seemed in memory to be cottage industries.

The first time I ever heard the term "cottage industry" it was part of a Peace Corps presentation. The term was used to describe a process whereby the day-to-day activities and products of a group of tribal people could be made in quantities sufficient for sale as income producing goods. Thus, a native tribe somewhere that made beautiful cooking pots would be encouraged to make more than they needed for their own use and sell the extras to generate income. In this way, these people would have money to buy some of the things they needed but could not produce themselves. Each native hut became a cottage factory with each family or person producing as much surplus goods as they could or wanted to.

After giving the matter some thought, I wondered if perhaps that really was a good description of family farming, as I knew it. On our small Iowa farm, the first order of business was to produce the food and provide the shelter needed to sustain life in a sometimes harsh climate. By raising a large garden and canning tons of fruit and vegetables, my mother saw to it that we ate well and plentifully. The piles of wood that my father cut, and the wagonloads of corn cobs for kindling heated most of our 19th century vintage farm house.

The livestock raised on our farm provided meat, milk, and eggs. The surplus of each of these commodities went to Omaha or a local creamery and egg buyer to provide money for all the other things we needed.

It was a real family effort. The smallest children gathered eggs and pulled garden weeds. Older children milked cows, carried in wood or coal, and did other light farm work. The oldest children and adults did the heavy and dangerous work of handling livestock and raising field crops.

Farms were labor intensive industries, and labor we did. We got pretty good at it. On many post-WWII farms, the gap between survival and something called "profit" began to widen, and "agribusiness" was born.

Yes, I suppose we were a cottage industry at that, but it was from those little family farm cottages that emerged the skills and know-how that formed the basis for those big corporate operations. Furthermore, I'll bet that somewhere in the heart of one of those big successful feedlots, behind the corporate offices, desks, and computers, there is a "cottage" inhabited by a hard-working, competent farmer, providing for a family - a farmer who knows and really cares about all those corporate cattle.

A Midsummer Night's Misery

Years ago, before central air conditioning, there was the misery of a still night...
Hardly a leaf stirred on the big maple tree in the front yard.
The buzz of the locusts stopped an hour or so ago.
There was no use for bed covers on this August night. In fact, it was hot just lying here wearing only the barest necessities.
Iowa's heat and humidity lived up to their reputation today. It was a battle to keep the hogs out of the mud holes that used to be the crick running through the pasture. The desperate animals finally had to be locked up and the hog yard watered down to keep them cool. Farmers lose lots of ready-to-market hogs in those mud holes on hot days. They just pile up on top of one another searching for a cool, damp spot. The animals on the bottom suffocate in the process.
But now it's dark.
The squeals of misery are quiet.
Slap, slap, slap, slap.
The lids on the Pride of the Farm feeders drop as the hogs eat while it's cooler...in the dark.
The dog gets off the front porch. The clink of the house yard gate... a couple of barks over the platform fence just to let those stupid hogs know she's in charge.
Some scuffling of hooves and the clank, clank of the back oiler - the fat steers in the cattle yard are moving around in the quiet...in the dark.
The day was spent in the shade of the shed dozing and switching flies.
Nighttime. Cooler air. Time for eating and drinking - and scratching one's back.

A bark or two at those restless cattle and the dog heads back to the house.

Click, click of toe nails on the wooden porch. Clunk. Sigh. Back to dozing and watching.

The air is too still for windmills. Across the road, a neighbor's pump jack pushes water up to the farm place - pop-chicka-pop-chicka-chicka-pop-pop-chicka. The little hit-and-miss John Deere engine counts its curious cadence in the deep dark of the summer night.

Some screech owl parents escort their brood of chicks out for some nighttime hunting. With quavering voices they call to one another from their perches on the house yard fence posts. They're only fluffy little birds, but the cries have sort of a lonesome, eerie sound.

Silence. The owls took their hunting elsewhere.

Squeak, squeak. The bed springs protest the search for a cooler spot. Perhaps the other side of the pillow...

Bzzzzzzzeeeeee. Oh, fine... a mosquito in my ear.

With a whir and a gurgle, the old Frigidaire downstairs labors to keep its contents cool. A real challenge, but it manages.

A rustle of maple leaves and just the slightest hint of a breeze...no...maybe...wishful thinking.

Quiet. Dark.

That sun will be hot already when it comes up.

Maybe we'll get at least a couple of cool hours to sleep.

Maybe.

Not Really Fall

The case could probably be made
That fall began each year
The day the calendar would say
That shorter days were here.

One certainly could argue that
When frost would paint the grass
And sparkle on the pumpkin shell,
That summertime was past.

It's true enough that falling leaves
In colors bright and bold
Against a blue October sky
Meant soon it would be cold.

The flying "V's" of southbound geese
Would thrill us with their call.
And silence fell, the birds were gone,
That proved it! It was fall.

The day the wood stove was set up
To chase the morning chill,
We had to finally admit
That fall was here, but, still...

There was one final sign required
As proof when all was said,
It wasn't really fall until
OUT CAME THE FEATHER BED.

That last confirming sign was met
With feelings of delight.
Who cared about the frost? We'll sleep
In "feather ticks" tonight.

That fluffy mound upon the bed
Brought comfort just to see,
The winter's howling, freezing blasts
Would never get to me.

One had to break it in just right
Before the first night's sleep.
To land dead center was the goal
With one great flying leap.

So, properly prepared and safe,
In comfort, foot to head,
We welcomed fall, because our mom
Got out the feather bed.

M-O-O-O-M-M-M.
What's there to do?

It's midwinter in Iowa.
It's cold outside. There's snow on the ground.
It's Saturday morning.

Most homes don't have televisions yet, so Saturday morning cartoons are no solution.

What's there to do?

Lots of moms over the years have needed to respond to that plaintive wail of a bored child in bad weather. Today, television sets and the Mighty something-or-other Power Rangers or the Teenage Mutant Ninja Turtles often become the solution. Perhaps a video game, CD, or other electronic entertainment will fill the bill. Not so in the days before television. Other answers had to be found.

If the weather wasn't bitter cold, and if the right kind of snow was on the ground, sledding was always a first option. Even though today the idea seems kind of hazardous, the best place for sledding was the road running past the farm. A good snow pack on that hill would produce some fine trips on the steel runners of my American Flyer. With brother and sister similarly equipped, every trip down the hill was a race. A late winter ice storm provided some real thrills as the sleds hit supersonic speeds down the glazed road. For an extra effect, a final run down the hill at dusk would produce an intermittent trail of sparks as the runners nicked the tips of large bits of gravel poking up through the snow base. Of course, you always had to be on the lookout for a neighbor with a pickup load of hog feed, but there are prices to be paid for all pleasures. When there wasn't sufficient snow on the road, one or two half-slide-half-crash tumbles down the high cut bank along the roadside were enough to send us looking for another diversion.

Sometimes that meant a trip to the barn for a game of basketball. In our younger years the basket was the square sliding cover off the outside of a livestock mineral block. Nailed to the barn wall above the wooden floor over the horse barn, the box was just slightly larger than the small basketball. Your shots had to be right on. The tight fit between basket and ball left no room for error. While challenging for a while, the demand for precision shooting soon left us looking for another way to pass the time.

Often that meant building a snow fort. In rural schools as well as on farms or in town, the right kind of snow meant building snow forts. Sometimes it was simply a wall built from round balls rolled in the wet snow. Sometimes it was more sophisticated with a roof supported by old boards and walls built from square blocks carved from hard, late winter snow banks. Whatever the building technique, each snow fort was an architectural triumph. Sometimes the forts became havens of refuge during snowball fights, or they became impromptu clubhouses for the neighborhood gang. Sometimes they were just something to make on a snowy winter day.

If the cold was just too bitter, or the snow was wrong, or if we were just tired of outside games, we had to entertain ourselves inside. The old Victrola phonograph upstairs was usually good for a day or so. The brittle old black records with the funny sounding songs provided many mornings' worth of entertainment. I suspect my mother could have happily gone whole winters without hearing "Listen to the Mockingbird" or "Hallelujah, I'm A Bum" one more time.

When our musical tastes had been satisfied, it was time to go for the tried and true. Uncle Wiggly board games, a round or two of Old Maid, a couple of throws at the Hop-along Cassidy Lasso game, or some time at the cork pistol shooting gallery never failed to provide an hour or two of fun.

Now, lest I give the idea that this was altogether the Stone Age, let me assure you that we weren't totally without electronic entertainment in those days. From WOI in Ames came the "Children's Happy Tune Time" in mid-afternoon. Perhaps that was the forerunner of today's Sesame Street. For something a little less educational, Saturday morning featured Smilin' Ed McConnell and the Buster Brown Gang ("Plunk your magic twanger, Froggeee.")

Sigh, now that was real entertainment.

When is a River Not a River?

When it's a crick.
Not a creek, mind you, but a crick. Creeks are little, clear, sparkling fountains that babble down mountainsides. Cricks are muddy, cloudy streams that loiter their way sluggishly through field and pastures.

Its real name is the Nishnabotna River, but usually it's just called "the crick." If you told a Manning resident you were going fishing in the river, they'd probably think you were headed for Omaha or up to Rainbow Bridge. However, if you were going fishing in the crick, "Why didn't you say so?"

We had several cricks on our farm. There was the one behind the grove and the crick down by the windmill; not to mention the crick down in the pasture; but there was only one real crick.

Whose crick or which crick kind of depended on whose land it flowed through. There was Hagedorn's crick with the beaver dam, and Alvan Hansen's crick, and Wilbur Hill's crick where they found the Buffalo skull, and Kusel's crick. Tony Muhlbauer had a crick; and since the thing started up by Fred Grau's place, maybe it was Grau's crick.

Whoever crick it was or is, it's always been a part of the Manning area. Kids have floated on it, trapped in it, skated on it, and gotten muddy in it. Farm cattle have gotten a drink from it. It has been frozen solid enough to walk on, dry enough to walk across, and swollen into a destructive, quarter-mile-wide battering ram after a summer thunderstorm. It's been straightened, dammed, cursed, enjoyed, and polluted; but it's always been the crick.

And somewhere, in a yet undiscovered spot, lurk a couple of those big catfish that many have tried for and few have caught. It's not mighty, famous, or necessarily picturesque. But sitting beneath one of the old railroad bridges fishing for bullheads was adventure enough for many on a summer's day. One hopes there will be a crick to fish in and a bridge to sit under for a long time to come.

You Can't Get There From Here

Manning never boasted a Fisherman's Wharf or a Chinatown. We had no landmarks like Pike's Peak, Mount Hood, or Mount Rushmore. We didn't have any road signs with colorful names like Wall Street or helpful numbers like "County Road 29." Maybe that's why Dad wound up escorting the two lady strangers with the out-of-county license plates down the lane through the cornfield and out of the hayfield where they had finally wound up. To the distraught strangers, one little narrow road probably looked just about like another. This one did seem to be a little bumpy, but then again, out here in the country…

To the uninitiated city dweller, the one-mile grid of gravel, asphalt, or plain dirt roads was like a giant maze from which one was lucky to escape, especially since there were no directions, signs, or landmarks to follow.

You see, it was all very confusing unless you knew where Parker's corner was. No matter if there were no Parkers living there, it was still Parker's corner; and there's the point – we all knew where we were going, they were the ones with the problem. Why, any Manning area person would have had no trouble at all, but one can imagine the glaze in the eyes of a foreigner (from Des Moines or some other distant place) at the suggestion that, "It's easy, all you have to do is go past Parker's corner, along Wilbur Hill's bottom, over Heinie Hansen's hill, turn left at Herbie Bruhn's corner, past Carl Schrum's pond, and over Bill Brus' hill." By the time the kindhearted and helpful Manning resident got to Wilbur Hill's bottom, the visitor was ready for a stop at Grimm and Vinke's for a quick one to steady the nerves.

Even locals who were pretty well used to the system would occasionally get bogged down at the "old Opperman place" or some other reference to a farm or corner where no Opperman had lived in recent memory.

When all else failed, strangers would be given some real precise reference points such as "one half mile past the railroad tracks to the farm with the blue silo," or "You can't miss the big brick corncrib." This assumed, of course, that the wanderer knew what a corncrib was.

Beyond these obvious references, some area landmarks were christened with more colorful names by individuals who had a special interest. Glidden Creamery truck driver, Les Reisberg, dubbed Bill Brus' hill "Mount Moses" after battling a few winter runs up its slope. One certain local peak was referred to as "Big Hill" by high school students directing others to certain recreational activities.

So, there you have it; if you knew where Parker's corner was, or could find the Five Mile House road or the Three Mile House corner, you were in business. It all makes "Interstate 80 at the Elk Horn exit'" seem kind of unadventurous by comparison.

If These Bricks Could Talk

There are brick streets all over the U.S. Small towns as well as big cities throughout the country have brick streets. A paving project on Salem, Oregon's State Street uncovered a long forgotten brick street surface in which streetcar tracks were laid. Brick streets in themselves are not particularly unique.

Brick streets all hum, or rumble, or whatever you call that sound when you drive over them. Over the years of use and street improvements, Seward, Nebraska, has left several blocks of brick streets that sound more or less like Manning's as the car tires roll along. Brick streets that hum are not in themselves particularly unique.

But Manning's brick streets are the best! Manning's brick streets don't hum, or buzz, or rumble - they sing! At least, lots of us who grew up there think so. Somehow, those brick streets hold a special significance in the memories of many Manning natives. Just the sound of driving on those bricks is enough to trigger special memories. Those bumpy, uneven, red bricks seem to be connected with all that is or has been Manning.

Ah, if those bricks could talk...

They might talk about all the Saturday nights. They'd remember how all the farm families came to town from miles around. Sometimes you couldn't even find a parking place on Main Street. All the parents would visit and all the younger kids would "make the rounds" by walking the length of one side of the street, cross over, and walk the other direction down the other side. The boys would walk one direction, the girls the other - all the better to see one another as they passed.

The bricks might shudder a bit as they remember the loud mufflers or "cut-outs" rumbling as the older kids "drove around." Back and forth from the Petersen Garage/Manning Motor corner north to the Loucks building; they would make a U-turn (with just enough tire squeal to show off but not enough to attract the attention of the town police). Then, they'd head back south to the other intersection, with another U-turn and on and on.

The old bricks might tell the story of that one particular Saturday night when Ronnie Hiatt raced from the Council Oak Store to the hospital with an injured child in his arms.

Or they might tell of the scorching heat they felt on the night when Rix's Feed Company (where the city offices now stand) burned down or the night when the old fire station and library burned.

Surely we might forgive the red bricks if they remind us, with a touch of pride, that they have served five generations of Manning residents. They've seen babies-in-arms grow up to become grandfathers and great-grandmothers. With a little gloating, the bricks might remind us that they have survived the tests of time: iron shod horse hooves, Model Ts, terrible winters, tire chains, four-wheel-drive pickups, rain storms, and the heat of Iowa summers. In the meantime, that marvel of modern highway construction, Interstate 80, has been repaved twice in its 35-year lifetime.

The bricks could tell us that their lifetime has spanned the time when Manning had passenger train service at the Great Western Depot, when Manning's airport had a hangar with airplanes in it, and when Manning had regular bus service that loaded and unloaded passengers in front of the Virginia Cafe.

Oh yes, the bricks have seen and could tell of fender-benders, including one involving this writer and his date the night of the Junior-Senior banquet 1958. But...if the bricks could talk you'd have a hard time getting them to whisper anything they might know about other incidents such as Manning's famous "murder mystery."

But the bricks might most happily remember the parades. What a joyful sensation! Every Children's Day - the patter of hundreds of young feet, the jiggle and shake of dozens of strollers and coaster wagons, the laughter and chatter of grandparents on the sidewalk, and perhaps the grade school band. The crisp autumn brought Homecoming at Manning High School. The Homecoming parade featured the Bulldog band marching proudly in uniform, entries from commercial supporters, and marvelous floats constructed from hayracks, chicken wire, napkins, and excitement. For a few years it was "Industrial Day" when many of Manning's businesses hosted open houses for the day, and those riding on the parade floats tossed candy and other goodies to the crowd lining the streets. And the Grand Daddy of them all (or, in current language, the Mother of all Parades, since great big things have somehow changed gender) was the Centennial Parade when thousands watched parade entries tell the story of Manning's first 100 years.

Perhaps, if they thought hard enough, the bricks might tell of their beginnings, when two men with black skin and an African heritage laid the bricks with tremendous skill – a contribution from a different ethnic heritage.

A person might be rightly chided for painting an over-romantic picture of these few blocks of slightly uneven, easy to trip on, never really very smooth streets, but as some of our lives have led us to come and go from Manning over the years, we might make the case that the most enduring sight or sound of our home town is our brick Main Street. May the bricks talk, buzz, hum, or rumble, or whatever it is that they do, for many years to come.

It's All About Caring

The old Pillsbury commercial had it about right:
Nothin' says lovin' like something from the oven.
The commercial writers tapped into something very basic in the human makeup - the connection between the preparation/offering of food and the perception of love. One need only listen to the language of hospitality. "Would you stay and have a bite to eat?" "Have you had lunch yet?" "How about coming over for dinner on Sunday?" The connections are very strong and have a long history. The Bible is filled with stories of people eating together and many Christians find the "Lord's Supper" to be an especially meaningful event in their earthly pilgrimage toward the "Heavenly banquet." Charles Dickens' *A Christmas Carol* reaches its climax with the setting of a family gathered in warmth and love around the dinner table at Christmas. In the words of the Dickens character, Tiny Tim, "God bless us, every one," a connection is made between the loving meal and the blessing of God, Himself. American television drama caught the vision with the mealtime scenes being the centerpiece of such television dramas as "The Waltons" and "Little House on the Prairie."

At no time during the year is this connection between food and love more evident than at Christmas. Ask anyone what they like about Christmas and one of the things mentioned will certainly be food. More often than not the sentence will begin something like, "My mother used to make this incredible..." The *Manning Monitor's* Weihnachtsfest special editions used to feature recipes as a key ingredient in the celebration of the Christmas festival. Even a pronunciation guide has been included in order to help readers say the original names of those German holiday delicacies.

Stepping into the kitchen of our Iowa farm house after school during the holiday season was an experience like no other. The smell of baking was such powerful perfume. It drew us in like a magnet and prompted the immediate questions, "What are you making? Can we have one?" (We still needed a little work on grammar.)

It wasn't just the cold weather outside contrasted with the warmth of the old wood and coal range that created such a sense of welcome. That was only part of it. It wasn't just that we kids were half starved after a day of learning and playing at Ewoldt No. 2. That was only part of it. It wasn't just that at this time of year Mom really outdid herself in producing a quantity and variety of experimental and traditional holiday goodies. That too was only part of it.

No, it doesn't explain all that simply in terms of hunger, heat, and variety. It has much more to do with the sense of love, caring, safety, and human warmth that went with our farm house kitchen, especially at Christmas.

Christmas was a special time for us as it is even today for most people. There is a feeling about this time of year that is found at no other time. People often use the term "Christmas spirit" to describe it. That seems a little bit trite to me. Sometimes that phrase seems to represent something like a Christmas suit that one must pull out of the mothballs each year and wear for a few weeks to be in step with what's happening, and one is regarded as being somewhat odd if it's not being worn properly.

No, it's still more than that. The feeling of "something from the oven" is that expression of human love and care which touches the most basic of human needs and responds with "Have you eaten? Here, I have made something special for you." It is the step of holding out the hand of love before there is a need. It is love that makes the recipient feel very special.

For years a package arrived at our door shortly before Christmas. The return address of Manning, Iowa, was the tip-off that Grandma Ida had managed to again bridge time and distance and mail a little bit of that farm kitchen to her scattered offspring and grand-offspring in the far corners of the United States or even overseas. As welcome today as it was in college dormitories and military barracks, the package is the first item of that day's mail opened with a sort of treasure hunt atmosphere. What did she make this year?

Regardless of the variety of Christmas goodies in the box, one package has become symbolic of all the family experiences over the years and the relationships that have flourished as a result. The idea was best expressed by a college-junior-aged son within the hour after traveling 1,500 miles to return home for Christmas vacation: "Where are Grandma's peppernuts?"

Nothin' says lovin' like...

Hello From Omaha

"Hello from Omaha."
"It's a beautiful day in Chicago, and I hope it's even more beautiful wherever you are."
"Welcome to the Cornbelt Farm Hour."

For years the words and voices were as familiar to rural Americans as those of friends and family. Indeed, broadcasters such as Hart Jorgensen of KFAB, Omaha, and Frank Field of KMA, Shenandoah, Iowa, truly became friends to their listening audiences and shared their lives via the airwaves. These broadcasters weren't just announcers or news reporters. They took personal interest in the welfare of their audiences. They could probably come pretty close to identifying the counties of residence of lots of local names. They knew their listeners. They never "talked down" to them. They were neighbors.

Farm radio. For lack of a better term, it describes a key element in the development of agriculture, farm living, and ultimately, agribusiness through mid-20th century America.

For Iowa farmers who were separated by gravel roads and long days of hard work, who could be isolated for days at the whim of a snow storm, for whom college was not the first option that came to mind regarding the future of their children, and whose very survival meant learning better ways of producing and marketing, the radio was their teacher and market analyst. They could learn how to avoid certain diseases in their livestock. They would be given early warning about the likely outbreak of particular crop pests. During the growing season, they would get regular updates on how the crops of the farmers in other counties were doing.

For the men, it was both the Omaha market report and the livestock grapevine. "----------- from Audubon, Iowa, topped the market today at $27 with 30 angus steers weighing in at 1025. From North Platte, --------- brought in a nice load of 44 white face feeder steers at 415 pounds selling for $36 a hundred." The names and places became familiar over time.

For the women, radio offered household hints and home economics class. Home economists shared tips on everything from preparing meals to avoiding food poisoning by proper food care at a picnic. It was sort of a combination of Heloise and Julia Child. In an era which bridged the wood and coal "cook stove" to the electric and gas range and which ushered in the time of the home freezer (thereby creating hard times for the local locker plant), the "homemaker" radio programs were a learning link and the voice of another woman in the difficult and sometimes lonely world of a farm wife.

These were the years before the Internet was even an idea. Few television sets flashed their bluish light in farm windows at night. Long days left little time for reading much but the *Register* or the *World Herald*. Whether it was the Allis Chalmers-sponsored Cornbelt Farm Hour or Neil Trobak selling Purina Chows during the local "Interior Iowa and Southern Minnesota" market report, the radio linked, educated, comforted, and entertained a whole generation of rural Americans as no other medium.

Bringing in the Chickens

Summer is officially over. The Noon-day sun has lost most of its searing punch and has become more of a mellow glow. The fresh autumn morning has taken on crispness, hinting at colder days to come. The cool evening air gathers in the bottoms, so that walking down to the pasture to bring in the milk cows gives the odd sensation of descending into a chilly swimming pool of air. The buzzing of insects in the dry grass has stopped, as all preparations for winter are now complete. The flocks of blackbirds gathering since August have departed for warmer climates.

On such a day as this, Mom and Dad announce to their less-than-enthusiastic offspring that it's time to bring in the chickens.

On a still cool spring day, the chicks had arrived as downy, peeping babies, picked up from Grundmeier's Hatchery and carried home in ventilated boxes bedded with that curious woody straw. In a short time, the yellow chicks had feathered out and graduated from the heated brooder to the wide world outside the building from which they exploded in a frantic, feathery blizzard each summer morning when the door was opened. The young roosters had gradually disappeared from the flock to become the centerpieces for Sunday dinners, family picnics, and threshing meals. Now the flock consisted of mature, young pullets some of whom had laid their first egg and were ready to assume their destined role as laying hens.

On warm, late summer afternoons, such flocks of white Leghorns or Rhode Island Reds colored the farmyards and groves of many rural homes. In the evenings the flocks crowded into their now-too-small childhood homes or perched in the branches of nearby trees, sometimes becoming midnight snacks for hungry raccoons or 'possums.

Now it is time to gather and transport them to the laying house. Barney Mohr and Buzz Hargens have hauled last year's hens away to their final reward. The laying house has been cleaned and re-bedded. The roosts have been painted with creosote to deter lice and other insects, and the hen house is now ready for its new inhabitants. All that remains is to get those new inhabitants from their old home to the new. However, since flocks of chickens don't herd or lead too well, there's only one thing to do.

To the unknowing, it would have seemed as if the devil himself had visited the farmstead for the evening. Loud squawks and cackles shattered the nighttime silence as the panic-stricken birds were grabbed and then carried by their feet, flapping and yelling across the farmyard to their new home. Blinking flashlight beams, snapping branches, yells of "Don't let them go! Hang on!", and the excited antics of the family dog came together to create a scene possible only in a tormented imagination. The tradition of bringing in the chickens continued.

While walking home from school one day, my sister and I, scavengers that we were, found an empty chicken crate along the road, perhaps lost from a passing poultry truck. After toting home our treasure, it occurred to us that we could streamline a really unpleasant task by combining our fabulous find with little brother Phil's Radio Flyer wagon. So, that fall, amidst a few dubious comments from Dad about making more work to avoid work, Bets and I moved our share of chickens in a somewhat calmer manner, thanks to the onset of the mechanical age.

Dad was a straight line thinker. "It's always worked, don't tinker with it," he would say. But, in his own time, he would, with suitable proof, accept useful innovation. He never said much about our chicken hauling system, but he'd evidently given the matter some thought. Some months later he returned home from a farm sale, and as he unloaded a newly purchased chicken crate, he noted that with two crates instead of one, we'd get things done a lot faster around here.

The Very First

In the Old Testament, much is made of the Hebrews' responsibility to give back to God a thanksgiving offering of the "First Fruits" of all their farming or herding efforts. It was understood that the First Fruits of any crop or enterprise had special significance and were therefore especially suitable for a gift to the Divine Giver of all Good Gifts.

Firsts of anything are special, electric, fleeting, and memorable. Think of that first love. No other was ever quite the same. Remember the first solo trip with the family car? How important and free and grown up we felt.

Ah, firsts. Others came later and were satisfying, fulfilling, and wonderful; but they were not the first. The thrill of firsts is a combination of anticipation, surprise, and newness. Firsts are also things to be treasured, and held, and savored.

In remembering the past, the clearest memories often involve firsts. In fact, the seasons of the year and of life are marked by firsts. Picture the moment you saw your first child-that tiny, fragile bundle that was now the very center of your life. The first day each year when we look at one another and say, "It really feels like spring today...the first morning when we hear the "cheer up" song of robins or sniff the first aroma of spring blossoms...these bring a thrill to our hearts that says, "Dark winter is past!"

Here are some firsts from my memory:

-The first frosty fall evening with a fire in the dining room heater. How cozy was that snap and crackle.

-The first cackling rooster of pheasant season.

-The first snow fall of winter, covering all the brown earth with clean white.

-The first Christmas carol on the radio each December. (Christmas preparations started a little later back then.)

-The first day of the spring thaw.
-The first day of summer vacation.
-The first evening frogs sang down by the creek each spring.
-The first whiff of fresh cut alfalfa hay.
-The first fried "spring chicken" from the flock.
-The first ripe apple off the old Duchess tree by the garage.
-The first roasting ear from the sweet corn patch.
-The first night in the college dorm knowing that an important corner had been turned.

Firsts...there are so many more: some happy, some not, but they were all significant. The first time you realized that you had left home for good. The first loss of a loved one to death. The first day of retirement.

The old Hebrews were taught the significance of firsts. They were to offer up their firsts as not just tithes to the church, but as remembrances of all the God-given moments of their lives that had all, once upon a time, been firsts.

Crickets in the Hay

In my mind, there's something gentle about the memory of making hay. It wasn't "baling" back then, it was "making hay." On a fair number of farms hay wasn't pounded into blocks, or rolled into rolls, or squeezed into pellets, but rather hauled loose in huge fluffy loads to the barn. It was a rather quiet process with only the sound of the lightly loaded tractor, or before that, the creak of horse harness to accompany the sound of meadowlarks singing on the fence posts. The hay was lifted from the windrow by an odd but ingenious contraption called – what else? A hay loader. Hay loaders were sort of rolling ramps with a set of mechanical rakes attached that pulled the hay up the ramp and dumped it onto the hayrack where someone would stack the hay, as the whole outfit - tractor pulling hayrack pulling loader - moved along the raked windrow of hay.

It was not a fast process. The tractor operator drove fairly slowly for the sake of the man on the rack who was in constant motion. It was hard work, bouncing along on a steel wheeled hayrack, knee deep in loose hay, stacking, pitching, and packing the load with a three tine pitchfork. It was clean work, although rained-on clover hay produced a messy, black, dusty fungus that could render a man unrecognizable in about two loads. It was also reasonably safe work. The ground driven hay loader lacked most of the mechanical hazards of more modern engine driven farm machinery, although a stab in the leg with a fork or a quick trip over the side as a result of a wheel hitting a badger hole were always possible. Even the bull snakes cooling off in the shade of the hay row were deposited alive, well, and squirming into the lap of the man on the rack.

Loose hay required more storage room than tightly packed baled hay. Even though the men in the barn stacked and tramped as well as they could, the barn filled quickly. Putting the hay in the barn was also a rather quiet process, as in our case, the big grapple fork bites of hay were pulled up into the barn by old Dan, one of a neighbor's two remaining draft horses.

Early in my life, more affordable and convenient hay balers changed all these things. We could make our hay faster, tighter, and neater, although the relative merits of loose hay vs. baled hay regarding "curing," nutritional quality, and even fire safety were long debated. It was progress of a kind, but I don't know if the music will ever be the same. Those quiet moments, after the last hayrack had been emptied and the thick hay rope had been pulled back into the barn, were filled with a special sense of having really accomplished something. The evening sounds of livestock around the barn and that incredibly rich and delicate aroma of newly dried hay provided atmosphere for the tired but satisfied conversation of men who had done what was needed for the day. And the final, happy touch for such a time was the symphony of music provided by the thousands of crickets that rode in with the hay and sang the day to a close.

They Got the Job Done

There were lots of different kinds of workers around Manning in the '50s. The town had mechanics, blacksmiths, hatcherymen, truckers, shopkeepers, cooks, farmers, printers, movie projectionists, and even a man who ran a popcorn stand. All these different workers contributed to a thriving, diverse, farm town economy.

There was another group of workers, without whom many of the previous folks' jobs would have been much more difficult. Most of these workers never owned a store or a business, never belonged to a union, or wore a fancy work uniform. Bib overalls, a white T-shirt, and a baseball cap were often their work clothes. Nothing fancy, but it got the job done. They had names like Deke, Barney, Clay, and Ernie. You name it, they had done it. They had dug ditches, pitched bundles, driven tractors, loaded cattle, swept floors, culled chickens, nailed shingles, painted barns, and shelled corn. The tools of their trade were wide experience, their hands, and their backs. They were day laborers.

Don't get the wrong idea. It wasn't that they couldn't hold a job. Most of them had held a number of good, responsible, long-term jobs in their lives, but at the time I knew them they were day laborers. They worked at short-term jobs, and they filled a valuable slot in the Manning economy. Nothing fancy, but they got the job done.

When a farmer needed an extra hand for a couple of days, these were the men he called. If a feed or lumber company needed extra hands to unload a train car, this was the labor pool. When a hatchery needed an extra man to help cull a farmer's flock of laying hens…you guessed it. Maybe the job lasted an hour, maybe a day, maybe a week; but it had to be done. The call went out. A phone call or a stop downtown usually took care of the need.

High school or college age boys occasionally became part of the same work force, and when I was a college student home for the summer, I got to know Clay.

It was not the kind of work I'd like to, or would be able to do today. Eight hours a day of wielding a pick and shovel in preparation for pouring concrete into broken sections of street and sidewalk. Clay must have been nearly 50 years old at the time, and he taught me about day labor.

Clay drank too much. Everyone knew him as a hard drinker. I heard various stories about his life and how he got started drinking. I don't know which, if any, were true. It's really not very important anyway.

I just know he beat me to work every morning. Not much was said, "…be another hot one today." When boss, Ed Hinz, came with the tools and the day's instructions, we'd probably just be sitting silently, enjoying the morning while it was cool.

One morning, I found Clay already swinging a pickaxe. Overnight, some local comedians had troweled our gasoline "bomb" flares into some newly poured concrete down behind the Loucks building. As I griped, Clay simply, without a word, grabbed a pick and went to work. Nothing fancy, but he got the job done.

Clay worked my arms off during those 90-degree August days. The pick or shovel in his big hands just never seemed to stop – except when the frequent groups of children stopped by to shyly ask, "Clay, do you have any gum?" Those hands of iron always found a pack of Wrigley's in a pocket, and to a chorus of "Thanks, Clay," "Bye, Clay." We went back to work. A mumble, "Kids, always underfoot" between swings of the pick. Children seem to have a sixth sense about a kind heart.

I don't think our paths ever crossed after that summer, but I consider one of my life's great achievements the fact that I was the only other day laborer who lasted that whole two-week job besides Clay. He could work!

Labor Day celebrations are little noted today. Many jobs formerly done by human sweat and toil are now done easily by machine. But, I'll stop for a second and remember Clay who taught me a lot about giving a day's work for a day's pay and sticking with a tough job.

Nothing fancy, but he definitely got the job done.

Who Knew it Would Be Valuable?

There are at least three unofficial "landfills" on our old farm place – three that I know of; there may be more. Very likely every former or present farm place in the Midwest has at least one. Usually the story went something like this: "That junk has been sitting in that shed (barn, basement, attic) for 10 (20, 50, only God knows) years. I'm tired of looking at it (we need the room, the kids are at school, and they'll never miss it), and it's not worth anything; so let's just bury it (dump it in the old potato cellar, throw it in the crick)." It all made sense, right? I mean, *who knew* that stuff was going to be valuable?

It is for this very reason that they come. They come from the big cities and small towns in cars, pickups, vans, and station wagons. With sweaty palms, fat wallets, and poker faces they scan the tables and hay racks at garage sales and auctions looking for the big buy, the great grab, the ultimate antique. Looking neither left nor right, they nod their bids hoping like mad that none of these local folks know what the thing is really worth in Minneapolis or Denver. Meanwhile the local folks are looking disinterested but inwardly wondering why those damn fools are bidding like crazy for that old piece of junk. "Why, we buried better ones than that," they thought. Who knew *that stuff* was going to be valuable?

Cleaned up and neatly arranged into homey little scenes or piled helter skelter on tables and shelves, the treasures in store are pretty things (old pictures, furniture, musical instruments and needlework), useful things (guns, feed sacks, tools, bottles, button hooks), and the obscure (window weights, corn husking hooks, cow hobbles, chamber pots) – all waiting to be discovered, bought and treasured.

Perhaps one of the kids had missed it after all. Perhaps a glimpse of the item in the antique shop window reminded a nostalgic former farm boy or girl of something or sometime pleasant. Sometimes it's just good for a laugh like the mint condition, enameled chamber pot in the antique store labeled as a "sweet corn cooker." Perhaps the item is just right for that spot over the mantle. "You're kidding! We paid less than that for a new one in 19--!" Who knew that stuff would be *valuable?* It wasn't – then. Nobody used those clamp-on ice skates anymore. Industrial progress was making the old items obsolete and America wanted "modern." Nobody worried about any overflowing city landfills, and nobody was concerned about recycling. The War was over, and there was no real need to gather or conserve metal. It wasn't even worth Harold Reinke's time and fuel to come out and pick it up. So we just buried it, or burned it, or threw it into unused potato cellars or washed out creek beds to help control soil erosion. If one hung a big enough magnet over Iowa, I'll bet you could unearth half the state with just the hand-cranked cream separators alone. That's why the few remaining cream separators (button hooks, horse collars) are so valuable; we buried all the rest. *Who knew?* I mean, you can't keep everything.

How Many Ways?

In our modern age of recycling, true genius is often revealed in the process of taking a second look at something that currently has no particular use or value - junk - and finding a new, practical, and even profitable use for it. Years ago, when nearly all corn was picked and stored on the cob, the final step in the process was to remove the ear corn from the crib and shell off the kernels. When the corn shelling machine left the crib, and the shelled corn was moved to a closed bin, what was left? You had a little mound of corn husks and a big mound of corn cobs. (Although most folks who were smart elevated the cobs right into wagons or a truck. Did you ever try to shovel corn cobs off the ground - off grass or weeds? I believe it was at such a point that I first thought of going into the ministry.)

Okay, so what can you do with a couple wagon loads of corn cobs?

Fifty years ago you might shovel those nice, dry, clean corn cobs into the cob shed for future use as fuel for the farmhouse kitchen range or heating stoves. Besides being pretty good kindling for wood, corn cobs themselves made a very good fuel for cook stoves. Corn cobs burn cleanly and evenly. They don't make a lot of ash, and they burn down nicely into a glowing bed of coals just suited for certain kinds of baking. ("Pig cobs" were an often used variation on this theme. The cobs were bigger and were picked up from hog feeding areas where the animals had been fed whole ear corn. ...Don't believe me kids? Ask your grandmother.) Many a farm wife knew just how many handfuls of cobs it took to bake a summer pie, and many a farm child had, as part of their chores, the task to "bring in a basket of cobs for the kitchen stove."

Occasionally, that wagon load of corn cobs was fed through the large screen on a "hammer mill" grinder and loaded into another wagon as roughly ground bedding for chicken barns. The ground cob mulch made an excellent deep floor covering for laying barns. The ground cobs would insulate the floor from cold, had excellent moisture absorbing qualities, and when applied in a four- to six-inch layer, provided the cooped-up birds with a place to scratch and exercise during the long winter. Shoveling this marvelous material out of that same laying barn after a few months was another story.

During the mid winter, the wagon loads of cobs might be hauled into cattle feedlots to provide a solid standing area for the cattle when the bottom went out of the dirt feedlot along with the frost during the spring thaw.

The corn cobs were even edible by livestock. Whole ear corn was often ground and fed with supplement to feedlot cattle in the earlier stages of fattening.

What a piece of raw material - the noble corn cob. At one point, a man from Manning would even haul your cobs away for free if you had no use for them. He was able to sell them and make a profit!

Nonetheless, corn cobs weren't "all work and no play." Mix together one large diameter corn cob, a six-inch box elder twig about as big around as your little finger, one Boy Scout pocket knife or its equivalent, one halfway skilled farm boy, and what do you get? A corn cob pipe, of course. The soft center of the corn cob hollows out nicely as does the center of a box elder branch. The hard part was drilling the hole through the outside of the cob in order to place the pipe stem. I think that may be where the locking-blade pocket knife was first thought of. Even in my younger years I never really tried to smoke one of those things, but it was probably possible.

An easier toy can be made by almost anyone. Three large bird feathers (chicken wing feathers) poked into one end of a two-inch section of corn cob can make a toy that works sort of like a badminton bird. A nail inserted into the opposite end from the feathers (with the pointed end in the cob) will add stability. When thrown, the toy will spin through the air for quite a distance.

Now, some of you are probably thinking of another reputed use of corn cobs. This use supposedly had something to do with outhouses. Stories abound, but I've yet to hear one based upon personal experience. 'Nuff said.

While most of these uses aren't applicable to my current suburban lifestyle, one use is still very relevant. Dry corn cobs make excellent scrubbers and cleaners for garden tools. In years past, corn cobs were often the tool of choice for cleaning cultivator shovels at the end of the day. Fathers knew that cleaning off the dirt prevented rust and taught sons to pay attention to the details of maintaining expensive farm machinery.

Maybe it's because I learned to keep my tools clean, or maybe it is a tiny link with my boyhood, or maybe it's because it keeps me in touch with the values and ideas of my creative ancestors - I don't know, but each fall I pull a few of those leftover "nubbin" ears from my sweet corn patch, dry them in the garden shed, and shell them during the winter. The birds like the corn, and I have a fresh supply of tool cleaners for the spring. Who says they don't make 'em like they used to?

It Doesn't Get Any Better Than That

Two events, in memory, stand out as a study in contrasts. One was big; one was small. One was impressive; one cozy. One in town; one in the country.

For all the contrasts, the two were the same. They celebrated Christmas and involved children. They both pay tribute to that wonderful tradition - the Christmas program.

Inside the little rural school building, the room looked very festive. Christmas drawings decorated the bulletin boards and walls. Red and green paper chains were draped strategically around the room. The white gas mantle lamps suspended from hooks on the ceiling hissed and glowed, providing light. The five rows of connected desks had been moved aside and stacked to make room for a stage area and chairs to seat the assembled throng of perhaps a dozen or so families. We would soon be treated to an evening of song, recitation, and home-cooked food. The program couldn't be too long. Since the school building was not equipped with electricity, and any food that arrived hot would soon get cold. The wood and coal furnace produced an ample supply of heat, and both the audience and performers were warm and comfortable.

Inside the high school gym, members of Zion Lutheran were ready for their Christmas program. The floor was set with row after row of folding chairs to accommodate the large group of people expected to attend. The decorations were limited to the one end of the gym, next to the stage. In Lutheran circles, the children's Christmas program was an important event. Often held on Christmas Eve, this particular program was held on another evening. That was always a topic of considerable debate. Some people felt strongly that Christmas

Eve was the proper night for the children's program, while others felt strongly that Christmas Eve was a time for families at home. Instead of the warm glow of lamps, the room was bathed in the light of overhead electric lights more suited for basketball games. The bleachers on the stage, which usually held the student rooting section, were now occupied by the Sunday school students waiting to sing their songs and "say their pieces."

The country school kids also sang songs and said their pieces. Mrs. Sander opened the evening with some well chosen remarks, and the program began. Larry and Darlene Genzen played a piano duet during the program. Yours truly recited a poem entitled "Jest 'fore Christmas" ("...I'm as good as I can be"). One singer forgot the words to her solo, but after a few tears and some reassurance, she performed admirably. Each student had a part in the program, but only Betty Ann Lengemann could pull this one off. "Hoowwwwdeeee! I'm just so proud to be hyer'. (That's "here" in Southern.) Minnie Pearl herself could not have done it better. It was star quality. All the students knew what the "big finish" would be. Some carols were sung, a few more recitations and then it was time for Santa (Where did Virgil Genzen go?) to arrive and distribute mesh stockings filled with candy and nuts. The school children gave handmade gifts to their parents, a few more "Ho, Ho, Ho's," and it was time to eat.

There was no eating at the Zion program. This was taken very seriously. For several weeks, the pastor and Sunday school superintendent had coached the delivery of memorized narration and Bible passages. The pastor especially wanted strong enthusiastic, loud singing of the songs assigned to the children. And when pastor wanted loud, he got loud. On the evening of the program all the children were dressed in their holiday best. With the gym half full of parents, grandparents, and friends, we knew we had to do well. This was an important part of the church year. Amidst the desire to be dignified and precise in the speaking of my lines was a secret joy. Often the speaking parts were done in duets. Naturally then, the two speakers had to sit side by side for the whole program. This particular year I was assigned a part with a girl whom I had been admiring from afar. YEEESSSSS!! God does indeed answer prayer! (Having already perhaps embarrassed Betty Lengemann, I'd better not push my luck. No more names will be mentioned.) I can still recite that year's Bible passage to this day.

The parents, grandparents and friends filed out of the gym in good German-Lutheran fashion. The children had done beautifully as expected. The grand story had again been told, and the tradition continued. Children's Christmas programs continue to touch the heart of those who attend and remember.

Back in the little rural school building, the coffee cups and pie plates had been packed away. The wrapping paper from the children's gifts had been collected and put in the wastebaskets with other scraps. We wanted to leave the building clean. Chatting parents and kids with laughing voices pulled on warm coats and boots in the now-chilly hallway of the school. The teacher and her family, who would be the last to leave, watched the families pile into frigid autos, cover up with lap robes, and drive away into the dark winter night to the farm places scattered across the sections around Ewoldt No. 2.

They were two greatly different events, yet very much the same. Friends and neighbors gathered around a common celebration, sharing their various gifts and talents, and bringing the warmth and care of community into one another's lives.

It doesn't get any better than that.

Under One Roof
Barns, Part I

If the farm house was the center of family activity on Iowa family farms, then the hub for the rest of the operation was surely the barn. The barn was to livestock what the house was to the human farm dwellers. It was a place of shelter, a place to find food, a place to work, and a place to socialize.

Most Midwest farm barns were designed to be far more than just a place to store hay. Barns were built to be the center of family farm livestock operations. They were in fact built to be small, self-sufficient communities, designed to provide a variety of services for a variety of animal and human needs. Small, post WWII family farms were highly diversified. Farm income was produced through a wide range of crop and livestock growing activities. Thus, barns had to service a number of different needs.

Essentially, barns of this era were central feed storage areas surrounded by animal feeding and shelter areas, all under one roof. A typical barn consisted of a large haymow capable of storing 50 to 100 tons of hay for feed and straw for bedding. Most barns also held one or more built-in granaries designed to hold small grains, shelled corn, or a variety of ground or bagged animal feeds. Surrounding these storage areas were feeding and shelter sections for livestock. The "cow barn" (even though in the same building, individual areas were often referred to as separate barns) held stalls, feed boxes, mangers, and milking equipment for the family dairy herd which consisted of one to perhaps a dozen cows, usually milked by hand. The "horse barn" was designed to meet the needs of the animals which provided the horsepower for farm equipment primarily in the first half of the century. The horse barn was also equipped with stalls, feed boxes, and places to store harness and tack supplies. With the passing of horse farming, many horse barns were converted to machine sheds or other uses. However, if a person walks into an old long-converted horse barn, they can still detect that familiar odor long after its half dozen teams of original inhabitants have been replaced.

The largest of the livestock areas was often the "cattle barn." Different from the cow barn, the cattle barn was home to non-dairy cattle, usually fat cattle from an adjoining feedlot. This was a simple space the length of one side of the barn. It held an end-to-end hay manger capable of feeding perhaps 30 to 50 cattle at one time.

Because of their great importance in family livestock farming, well designed and well built barns were valuable buildings. They had to be efficient in layout and durable enough to withstand many years of harsh Midwestern weather. Barns were therefore built with great care and much planning. Carpenters were chosen carefully for their abilities and experience in barn building just as home builders are chosen today.

Very few, if any, of these old style barns are built or even exist anymore. I only ever saw one barn built. That barn was on the Henry Sonksen place, currently being farmed by Karl Albertson. The barn was essentially laid out and built by one man, Fred Rutz. Fred was probably well into his '70s at the time. With help from the farm owner and hired man, the former barn was torn down and the new one, board by board, began to take shape. Each day, the blue Studebaker station wagon carried the craftsman back and forth from home in Manning to the job site. His sole calculating tool a carpenter's square, Fred brought the barn to life from laying out the foundation footings to nailing on the shingles. In mid-summer of 1956 the task was finished. The haying crew brought the first loads of hay into the new building. It was now properly a barn.

And then, only a few days later, that odd green cloud appeared on the morning horizon. The Manning area was devastated by that awful storm, and the new barn was in ruins. But neighborhood and community overcame even this. With the help of a crew of neighbors, Fred Rutz measured and eyeballed, directed and encouraged; and in one day the barn was almost completely rebuilt. As the crew of volunteers said goodbye and headed home to do evening chores, there was a sense that things would be all right now – the barn was back up.

Except in winter
Barns, Part II

Old barns are interesting. Artists paint pictures and photograph them. Authors write books about them – retracing their construction and history. An old country song tells the story of a young man's education "Out Behind the Barn."

What is it that makes barns so interesting? Perhaps it's something about the way they look that says, "Life." "Something went on here." Maybe it's their sheer size, or all the different shaped doors and windows that hint of interesting happenings. Whatever it is, barns have it. You may see an occasional artistic rendering of an old farm house, but I've never seen a painting of a hog barn or corn crib and only an occasional chicken house. Barns definitely have the edge.

I suspect that whatever sparks the interest, old barns seem to compel a person to wonder, "How was it back then for the animals that lived here and the people who cared for them?" The key word is **lived**. Barns were places where things didn't sit; they **lived,** each one in its place, going about its business.

From the skunks that lived under the granary floor to the pigeons that roosted up in the rafters, barns were full of life. The grains and hay attracted rats and mice which in turn attracted skunks and fed the barn cats (not to be confused with back porch cats, as anyone who has ever tried to pick one up will tell you).

Birds seemed to like barns. Pigeons, sparrows, and those pesky starlings came to squabble, peck, and raise their young in the barn's friendly nooks and crannies. One bird book states that "It is not clear where barn swallows lived before the coming of the farmer." The barn swallows feasted on the abundance of flies as did those disgusting hard-shelled spiders that lurked in the corners.

Not all these tenants were welcomed by the farmers. Many of the birds, as well as the occasional family of raccoons or 'possums, were evicted for the sake of cleanliness or just nuisance value...except in winter.

In the winter, a kind of informal truce seemed to be in effect. It was as though all within recognized their common enemy outside and respected one another's struggle to survive the harsh Iowa weather. In my memory the barn in winter was a friendly, warm place. With all the granaries filled, the haymow packed, and the outside walls of the cow barn insulated by a stacked layer of straw bales, the barn was almost cozy compared to the biting cold outside.

The barn cats crept near sleeping cows to take a bit of warmth from their big bodies (with occasional casualties resulting from a cow's sudden position change). Horses and feedlot cattle lounged in extra deep layers of straw bedding. Indeed, the end of each day's chores was a final check to see that everybody had enough feed and dry bedding for the night. On those real bad nights, the pigeons, sparrows, and even those pesky starlings roosted undisturbed. Nobody should have to be outside in this weather.

No, those aren't just quaint old buildings. They are symbolic of a certain time in rural history. They are symbolic of the diversified family farm that sometimes seems as antiquated and stereotyped as "Old MacDonald." They're also symbolic of a partnership of people and animals that depended upon one another for their livelihood.

I know family farms still exist, and I hope these farms have a place where it all comes together, a place where individuals recognize their need for one another and have the opportunity to demonstrate their love and concern through caring deeds – just like that old barn – especially in winter.

Here's to You, Howard Cosell

It seems very unlikely that Iowa will ever make a serious bid to host the Winter Olympic Games. While there is usually ample snow, ice, and cold weather, it does stretch the imagination a bit to envision a bobsled run or a ski jump on even some of the biggest hills around Manning.

Over the years, however, Midwest residents have found ways to take advantage of the abundance of winter and have enjoyed their own "winter games." The first blanket of snow on many schoolyards became a huge game board for a lively round of Fox and Goose. If the snow was wet enough, snow forts, snowmen, or snowballs usually began to appear.

Certainly downhill skiing and snowboarding take a high degree of skill, but Iowa sliding took its own brand of skill. It might be fun to see a snowboard expert try some of those fancy moves on a number 14 aluminum scoop shovel down a steep bank as some of us did in our youth. Sledding was always good, but an Iowa ice storm could turn a country hill into a bone rattling adventure. A steel-runnered Flexible Flyer that handled like a Porsche on packed snow had a mind of its own on a trail of glazed ice.

Beyond these semi-normal activities, there have been some lesser known sporting events that provided real winter thrills.

DOOR KNOB YELLING - also known as Taste Bud Roulette: This sport was practiced mostly in older, drafty two-story houses. It consisted of placing one's tongue onto an icy cold doorknob and then yelling like mad when the tongue was ripped loose from its frozen trap.

HAYRACK SPEED SKATING: This was generally done in very cold weather by livestock farmers carrying a bale of hay along a hayrack bed while wearing snowy overshoes.

MILK PAIL SHUFFLE: This was a type of figure skating done by carrying two full pails of milk or other liquid across a dark farmyard on a frozen path between snowdrifts. Perhaps this sport was connected with the origins of the old saying "crying over spilled milk," although crying was only one of several verbal options.

HOGYARD HOP: Similar to the Milk Pail Shuffle, this sport was played on icy livestock yards with additional landing hazards.

Where was ESPN when we needed it?

A Basketball Town

There wasn't a seat left to sit on,
The folks were packed in like sardines.
A yell shook the place when our boys took the floor;
Oh, this was a basketball town.

Bill Steneker's boys lit the fire
On that winter night in '48,
When they beat all the odds and became the State Champs,
And they made this a basketball town.

That was really a tough act to follow
For the fellows who played later on.
The great expectations, the hopes, and the dreams
Had fired up this basketball town.

Each boy who had gone with his father
To see Manning's Bulldogs compete
Had his goal set before him so lofty and high,
To play ball in this basketball town.

As the Sectionals led into District
It was just a cakewalk for our boys;
But the tough ones like Carroll and Glidden now loomed
To challenge our basketball town.

With the final plateau now before us,
The appearance of ghost town was seen;
For to State tourney games half the populace went
From our fired-up basketball town.

No, the feat has not once been repeated,
Tho' the victories many have come
To the teams and the coaches of old MHS
Through the years in this basketball town.

But, no matter if only one trophy
Of such status rests on the shelf;
There's little regret to be found anywhere
In the hearts of this basketball town.

There have been some radical changes.
Lady Bulldogs now share in the joy
Of competing, and winning, and taking the bows
And applause in this basketball town.

Yes, the trip has been certainly worth it,
And we've all had our share of the thrills…
Take a look at that kid! He must be six foot nine!
One more time! …in this basketball town.

A Fine Line Indeed

There is a very fine line,
Indeed,
Between a flower
And a weed.

I don't think my father really wanted them destroyed. We never sprayed them like we did the Creeping Jenny, Morning Glory, and Leafy Spurge. There never seemed to be any of the "Mortal Enemy" relationship that there was with Cockleburs, Sour Dock, or Canadian Thistle. After all, they weren't the terrible nuisance of Horseweeds in an oats field or even volunteer corn in a bean field.

It simply came down to this: every year, on a midsummer day, usually following overnight rain, it was declared that this would be a good day for "one of you kids" to go down to the cow pasture and "stick off those pretty thistles."

Actually, it seemed like a conflict in terms. Most thistles just aren't pretty – they're a nuisance. They're weeds. They'll grow almost anywhere. They take up crop space, scratch your legs, and pollute grain and hay fields. At one time they caused incredible anguish to any bare-handed oats shocker who grabbed hold of a bundle containing dried Canadian Thistles. Two or three thorns under a fingernail produced withering pain and could even lead to infection. "Pretty" thistles, indeed.

But, the thistles that grew in our cow pasture *were* pretty. The thick, succulent plants were a frosty green-white, and crowning their man-high top was a striking cap of intense, deep purple down. I never did learn their true name. To us they were simply "those pretty thistles."

I think it was because of their beauty that we never made a serious attempt to eradicate them. Sticking off the perennial plant with a spade did nothing to prevent it from growing back the next year. We all knew a few shots of kerosene down the hollow tap root would have spelled its doom, but we never did that. We simply cut them off every year, right after they bloomed. After all, you can't let them go to seed.

In a weak moment my father even acknowledged that those eight or 10 plants weren't really hurting anything down there in the pasture. The cows ate around them, and we had no reason to grab them bare-handed. Perhaps the ritual of chopping them off satisfied the need to let the neighbors know that we were properly intolerant of weeds, or that we must wage at least token war against all thistles. Each spring they would return, mature, bloom beautifully, and then be chopped down to the root.

West of our farm house was a little triangular patch of land that had apparently once been a potato patch. Later, at various times, it had been a calf pen, 4-H hog pasture and a playground for our young brooder chickens. Regardless of its current status, each spring for a few days it became a glorious, golden carpet of dandelions. In my memory's eye, few sights can match the beauty of that giant flower garden on a sunny spring morning.

It's perhaps the memory of those pretty weeds that causes me to make my suburban neighbors so nervous each spring. I do indeed fulfill my neighborly duty and spray the dandelions in my lawn – right after a few of them have bloomed.

This year I will again dutifully deal with my weeds and keep my neighbors happy, but I'll let one or two plants go to seed. I'd hate to miss the sight of those bright gold messengers of spring glowing boldly against the green grass. You see, I still believe there's room in this world for "pretty thistles,"

...or some silky milkweed seeds sailing on a brisk, fall breeze,
...or wild roses blooming on a roadside,
...or clumps of Elderberry bushes down in the ditch,
...or even a couple of dandelions in the lawn.

I hope we don't make our world so neat that we wipe out all the things that make it interesting, and surprising, and fun, and even a little disorderly – like pretty thistles in a cow pasture...because...

There is a very fine line
Indeed,
Between a flower
And a weed.

You Know it's Spring

It's about the time of year when elementary school teachers start cranking out the "signs of spring" assignments. Pictures of apple blossoms and robins begin illustrating everything from school bulletin boards to newspaper ads. Yes, the signs of spring are evident.

All that robin and apple tree stuff is good and well, but the most reliable spring indicators in rural Iowa didn't bloom and never flew or sat in trees.

Back in the days before year 'round hog raising operations, early spring was farrowing time. With snow still on the ground and nighttime temperatures still falling far below freezing, the first hungry, squealing signs of new life began making their appearance in family farm hog houses (or hog barns, depending on local custom). Many a hog house window gleamed with light far into the March night as farmers, fortified with jugs of coffee, carefully supervised the birth of hundreds of baby Durocs, Yorks, Hamps, or Poland Chinas. Most of those hog houses were blessed with neither insulation nor central heating systems, so extra bedding, heat lamps, extension cords, and that new farrowing pen system, combined to preserve the life of every possible tiny pig. More than one farm family ate breakfast while sharing the kitchen with a box or bushel basket full of little, squeaking four-legged guests whose yearling mother had reacted to the pressures of motherhood by refusing to nurse or even turning with murderous intent upon her new offspring.

Later, but before the first farmer's disc bit into the cold April soil, the ground squirrels emerged from wherever it was they went during the winter. One of the sure signs that the frost was out of the ground was that shrill, birdlike twitter as the little striped animals climbed out of their burrows for a fresh breath of spring air. On a warm, sunny morning the still bare hay stubbles and pastures became playgrounds for the little squirrels as they chased and called to one another, stopping every so often to pop up in that vertical "take a look around" stance.

The surest sign that spring had truly arrived was the sound of frogs. From their winter hibernation in the mud of farm ponds, slews, and creek banks, frogs or toads emerged at their appointed time and filled the night air with a symphony of song. Biologists tell us all about territorial battles and mating calls, but it was music to me. I remember being outside after chores in the evening or coming home from somewhere and just stopping to listen to that sound that said, "Winter's over, winter's over."

I don't remember consciously talking to my children about this, but maybe some things are observed by all generations. Perhaps these sounds touch something way down inside our souls, connecting with ages past. Who knows. But I got my memory refreshed a few years ago when my son stopped in the front door upon his return from a high school function. A short pause and then, "Dad, I can hear frogs over in the ditch, now you *know it's spring.*"

Some of My Best Memories are Smells

Someone finally did a scientific study on the whole deal. Their conclusion - There is a strong connection between memory and the sense of smell. Do tell!

Anyone who has ever closed his eyes, smiled nostalgically and said, "Boy, that smell reminds me of my mother's kitchen," could have reached the same conclusion. It's basic; smells can bring back memories faster than almost anything.

My own theory is that smells are stored in the brain's memory bank in the form of picture frames. Those frames are the settings or backgrounds into which the memory paints visual images of the past. When kitchen smells strike your nose, your memory paints into that background pictures and sounds of your childhood kitchen. The scent of a certain flower may frame the mental picture of your childhood home or a spring day of play from your childhood. For me, the smell of lilacs brings some very pleasant farm memories into focus.

One of the pieces in my "Manning memories" file is an article penned a few years ago by *Manning Monitor*columnist C O Lamp in his "Past and Present" column. It was kind of a smeller's tour of Manning's Main Street. He recalled the smells that wafted from various businesses that had occupied Main Street over the years. One could almost shut his eyes and see the people and the places. Two of my sharpest memories of Manning are connected with the tantalizing smells that came from "Butch" Wentzel's Locker Plant and Valentine's Bakery. Another smell that is hard to forget is the potent one which drifted from Pacific Adhesives after a fresh load of blood was delivered.

Has a smell turned on your memory lately? What smell might really get your mental pictures going? Would it be newly mown hay, a new box of crayons, peppernuts, wood smoke, plowed soil, or even something like VICKS VapoRub?

It occurs to me that this smell and memory connection is pretty powerful. Why else would I live in a neighborhood that - on a few days each year - smells like a hog barn? Lots of people in our area of Salem, Oregon, complain about the "mushroom plant." This is a large complex of buildings about a mile east of our house.

Now, if you're not acquainted with mushroom farming, let me give you a brief explanation. Commercially, mushrooms are grown in drawer-like trays in dark, damp, heated buildings. Instead of soil, the trays are filled with a ground-up mulch of wet straw, some commercial fertilizer, and ...yup, fresh from the farm. The plant is usually not even noticed until the wind goes around to the east on a day when they're emptying the sheds and changing the mulch – then you notice!

Over the years, we've lived happily in this house. Periodically one of the neighbors will mention the wind direction and grumble about that -------- smell. Well, I just close my eyes, look at the pictures, and say, "Shoot, it's not so bad. It kind of reminds me of home."

One Man's Foolishness

I'm sure no one saw me on the patio of my mother's north Manning home that clear, early summer morning. If they did, they've been too polite to mention it and ask why a grown man was wandering around outside in his BVD's at the crack of dawn carrying a portable tape recorder. And since I've never received any unsigned letters hinting that certain photos might end up at the Monitor office should I fail to send money to a post office box, I assume no cameras were around either.

So, what in the world was I doing out there? To quote an Oregon acquaintance upon his return from a first-time visit to the Midwest: "You were right. The bird songs were magnificent. Our birds out here just sort of sit and tweet, but back there, those birds sing symphonies!"

The product of that morning's labor was 45 minutes of the finest taped background music a transplanted Iowan ever played over his office sound system. Photos are fine, and bird books are beautiful, but to hear those sounds again...martins and swifts calling to one another as they sweep the morning skies for a breakfast of insects, house wrens tossing their bubbling songs into the air, blue jays adding their piercing voices, a cardinal calling from his home tree up along the railroad tracks, mourning doves, crows, blackbirds, and a robin in every bush. It was a symphony to be sure, a musical carriage to transport a person back to Iowa, to childhood, and memories of the bliss of waking up, lying half asleep in bed, and listening to all the joyful sounds of a beautiful spring morning.

Well, all this poetic rambling aside, one of the great loves of my life has been the sound of bird songs. Growing up in Iowa provided a tremendous opportunity to get to know these feathered singers and their songs very well. Other parts of the country have birds for sure, but the variety found in the fields, fence rows, groves, and urban forests of Iowa is equaled nowhere I've ever lived. Catbirds, brown thrashers, bobolinks, and diksissals are birds unheard of in much of the country.

It may be that many of us who grew up in the bird country of the Midwest took our good fortune for granted. As we grew up and perhaps moved away from our home towns and farms, we forgot about those daily concerts that brightened our mornings, marked the seasons, and were part of that total memory of home.

It's only when we return to visit and awaken early to that glorious racket that we remember. We sit still and listen to the music that we haven't heard in such a long time. We want to hold that moment of sound and take it back with us to our current world.

Well, that's why I had my tape recorder. I figured, if I take pictures to look at, why not take recordings to listen to? Boy, have I had reason to rejoice in that decision. One man's foolishness is another man's music. That recorded Iowa morning has been the ideal background for lots of mornings in my office.

Now, if someone wanted to do me a real favor, there's nothing sweeter than the sound of a meadowlark singing from a pasture post...

My Little Train

It was as regular as clockwork. Every morning the little local train came rolling down the Great Western tracks from Carroll. The whistle on the single diesel engine carried for miles in the cool, post-dawn air. At that still moment, before farmers and tractors set out for the fields, when even the hogs and chickens were barely awake and beginning to rustle up some breakfast, you could hear the whistle: long…long…short…long…echoing down the Nishna bottom as the "Dinky" passed each crossing on its way. I used to lay awake and try to guess which crossing was being signaled by the early rising engineer.

Manning was a railroad town. At the time of my childhood, four railroad lines ran through the community. The railroads were the lifeblood of many towns like Manning. In the years after wagon trains and before diesel trucks, railroads supplied mail, baggage, freight, and passenger service, connecting the small communities of the largely rural Midwest. The railroads were a major link in the economic chain, holding farm and market, city and small town, people and products together.

But, many people's memories of the railroads are much more personal than economic. They remember trains hauling away produce - the results of a year's hard labor. They remember waiting for the train to deliver that first automobile or tractor to Manning's dealerships. They remember sitting soberly at the crossing, watching the drab troop trains carrying Midwest farm boys off to war in Europe or the Pacific. They remember seeing the big steam freight engines pulling strings of flat cars loaded with battle tanks and artillery pieces from East Coast factories to West Coast seaports during the Korean War. They remember riding the train to visit friends and relatives or greeting others who arrived in town by the same means. Perhaps they remember seeing the dozens of baby chicks dumped in panic from their boxes by the baggage car derailment in a local pasture.

Trains weren't just hardware, they were part of life. Lots of people over 50 years old have a train story they can tell. An aged lady in an Oregon nursing home told me how she used to ride a train from Arcadia to Carroll when she was a barely-20 school teacher. From our farm we could hear the steam locomotives starting up at one of Manning's depots. A slow chug...chug...chug...straining to move the long line of cars – the rapid-fire chug-chug-chug-chug-chug-chugas ... the big drive wheels lost traction and spun in a shower of sparks on the steel rails ... and the resumed chug...chug...chug... when the engineer applied sand for traction and the engine slowly pulled the train out of the station and accelerated toward its next destination.

In later years, when the breeze was right, we could hear the multi-unit diesel streamliners rolling along the double Milwaukee tracks through Manning. Slowing down a bit through town, the huge diesels roared and throbbed as the engineer hit the throttle, bringing the train back up to cruising speed into the open countryside.

Some of us who attended school at Ewoldt No. 2 even had the opportunity to ride on the last run of scheduled steam rail passenger service on the Great Western Railroad between Manning and Carroll. Thank God for teachers who recognize and use such significant events in teaching.

It was the end of an era.

But trains always sound best at night. The sound of train whistles at night is the stuff used in songs and poems. The vision of the train crew peering from the dim cab into the black night has a hauntingly romantic quality about it. It all seems larger than life.

But my train was life size – or even smaller. My little "Dinky" with its 10 or so cars, stopping at each town to pick up a few cans of cream or to unload a couple of small freight items, was a symbol that everything was operating as it should. The rattle of the wheels on the rails and the long...long...short...long...was a wake up call. "The train's on time. Let's get up and get going. We've got a new day ahead of us."

No One Lives There Anymore

It's real quiet these days down in the Nishna bottom where the Great Western and the Northwestern railroad tracks used to cross the OCO. No trains whistle their warnings as they cross the road. No chickens or cattle bolt to the other side of Hagedorn's yard at the rumble of the locomotive. There's no farmyard sound of chores being done or children at play ... just that curious squeak and pop of growing corn and the rustle of corn leaves shaken by a passing breeze. No one lives there anymore.

The east side of that mile is empty now - that stretch of OCO, the third mile north of Highway 141. Once a schoolhouse stood at the south corner, Alfred Ahrendsen's family farmed the place one eighth of a mile further north, and the Hagedorn brothers, Lorn and Alvin, farmed the place down by the tracks. Two farm places, a school, two railroads, animals, and people - all gone without a trace.

I'm glad to have grown up in that neighborhood. It was a far cry from what many a city person might have imagined rural Iowa to be. The farms were smaller and closer together. Neighbors weren't miles away as some might guess, but rather, they were often literally within shouting distance. From our farm place, we could hear Hib Eischeid grinding feed or hammering on a board somewhere. On a fall morning the cattle and hog calls of two or three neighbors were plainly audible in the cool, resonant, dawn air. No, we weren't isolated at all; we were a neighborhood.

But, time changes things. I don't know which is tougher to deal with for one who returns: the clusters of empty farm buildings or those naked fields where a farm place once stood. My parents used to refer to a clump of box elders and a leaning shed as the "old ---- place," but I never really understood. Often, my father would mention "all the empty farm places." I could tell by his voice that it really bothered him.

It's only now, more than a half-century in age that I begin to understand...no one lives there anymore.

Perhaps it's the pangs of nostalgia, those sad-happy memories of life and times gone by, or a sharpened sense of my own mortality that causes that little pain in my insides. Whichever or whatever the technical reason, it's hard to drive down the road past those corn and bean fields that now produce crops but once were homes inhabited by neighbors and friends.

Every year my harrow teeth or cultivator shovels would unearth something on the little knoll on our north "80", south of Hank Sonksen's place. Sometimes it would be a bit of wire, sometimes just a couple of nails, sometimes a piece of unknown farm implement – but every year, something. I asked Dad where all that junk came from, and he said that at one time there was a farm place on that little knoll. Another empty field, just part of a "bare 80." No one lives there anymore.

Spring Thaw, Country Style

It wasn't really very warm yet. It just seemed that way after all the bitter cold. Compared to single digit temperatures, this was positively balmy.

The day began with a bright sunrise that scattered little rainbows on the wall of the farm house as it shone through the beveled glass pane in the front porch door. There was the sense of promise in the air. The first sign of change was the drip, drip of water off the tips of icicles on the south side of the house. Slowly at first, then building to a steady shower of droplets, the icicles wept until, one by one, they loosened their hold on the rain gutter and shattered on the sidewalk below.

Slowly but surely the sidewalk emerged from beneath the layer of packed snow and ice. The down spouts on the house made little musical noises as the ice in the gutters surrendered to the sun's strengthening rays, and water trickled and dripped through the metal spouts.

The winter-hard snow banks softened at the warming temperature. Each low spot on the farmyard became a little river carrying melted snow down the lane, into the roadside ditch, and then off to the crick and beyond. Children became instant engineers, scraping together snow and slush dams to create lakes and waterfalls with only four-buckle overshoes for construction equipment.

Down behind the barn, a meadowlark tried out a few notes of his spring song. He probably knew in his bird heart that it wasn't really spring yet, but it was a day worth singing about. There was hope in the air.

Near the corncrib, a gang of sparrows got into a noisy spat over a bit of spilled grain revealed by the melting snow. Or perhaps it was the leftovers in the cattle feed bunk. Or perhaps it was just over a place to perch. Who knows? Sparrows just seem to enjoy squabbling on sunny, late winter mornings.

The cattle in the feedlot left the shelter of the barn to linger a while over the feed bunks or waterer. This was a time of respite between the days of fighting cold and snowdrifts and the days of wading knee deep in sucking mud when the frost went out of the ground. Both livestock and farmer got a bit of a breather before the next seasonal hardship.

A neighbor's pickup made its splashing way as the tire lugs cut through the snow-now-turned-to-slush. Very soon these rural roads, like the cattle yards, would become hazardous, muddy, and frustrating pathways. In some places the bottom would go out, creating a spongy sink hole that could throw a car almost out of control. But that was a few weeks off. For now it was just a little slush over a frozen base...not too bad if you took your time.

It would freeze again that night. The slushy roads and farmyards would again turn to ice. The sparrows and the cattle would retreat into the warm buildings. The meadowlark would take refuge in a strawstack or weedy thicket. Winter wasn't quite finished.

But all knew that winter's grip had loosened. It had thawed a little, and more sunny days were ahead. The promise had been made and it would be kept.

The Golden Globe Reward

What is it about pumpkins anyway? Virtually every fall photo, drawing, painting and calendar contains pumpkins.

Kids love 'em. If you want real excitement, just turn 20 preschoolers loose in a pumpkin field. Lots of people plant them – for what? I mean, how many pumpkin pies can one person make or one family eat?

They're even named funny. We used to call the big ones "cow pumpkins." I never did see a cow eat one. The pigs liked 'em though.

Pumpkins do have a long and distinguished literary history. A pumpkin is one of the featured characters in the classic *Legend of Slepy Hollow*. Earlier still, someone wrote about Peter, the pumpkin eater who kept his wife in a pumpkin shell. I never did get the significance of that.

City supermarkets haul in truckloads of the orange globes just to haul about half of them away after Halloween.

The great goal in the life of a pumpkin is to be poked full of holes, stuffed with a lighted candle, and used to scare the dickens out of little kids on Halloween.

Well, perhaps that is all a bit foolish, but it's intriguing that something as outdated and irrelevant to modern life should remain as such a powerful and universal seasonal symbol. Usually pictured with a corn shock and split rail fence (two more antiquated objects), pumpkins show up in Halloween literature, Thanksgiving Day church bulletin covers, and Peanuts comic strips.

Perhaps pumpkins are like Christmas trees, objects that have over the decades of holiday seasons become an automatic part of the sights and smells of a particular season. Perhaps the pumpkin pies, while served almost exclusively during the Thanksgiving holiday season, despite the year 'round availability of canned pumpkin pie filling, add a particular taste to fall as the smell of evergreen does to Christmas.

Every year we raised pumpkins on our farm. Usually planted in edge-of-field dead furrows or early season cornfield washouts, the dozen or so hills produced a profusion of vines, flowers, and fruit between the rows of maturing corn. Sometimes planted by Dad and sometimes by my sister, brother, and me, the pumpkin patch was a necessary part of our family's annual farm ritual. Following the last cultivation of corn, the vines were ignored until just before corn picking time each fall, when the mature vines were visited to harvest whatever fruit might have been produced in those little corners of the farm.

It is at this point that I think the pumpkin delivers its real punch: the impact that makes it such a symbol of the harvest season. Each year was a treasure hunt. The dry vines yielded surprising treasures of great globes of gold. Those tiny seeds became sprawling vines which in turn produced huge colorful fruits. What a powerful symbol of the bounty of the harvest.

With the wagon box or little brown pickup heaped full of gold, the return to the farm place was a triumph. It didn't matter that Mom would have had to bake for 20 years to use up one year's crop, and that most of the pumpkins would end up being sliced up with a corn knife and fed to the hogs; this was the first fruit of the harvest – seed to plant to bounty.

I still plant pumpkins. My wife makes a couple of pies each year and the rest become decorations, jack-o-lanterns or compost. Heaven knows we could live without that part of the garden. However, each fall as I pick my crop of pumpkins, I'm reminded of where all this bounty comes from and how little I actually had to do with making it happen.

You want *What* for Christmas?

The days of the Montgomery Ward Christmas Catalog as we knew it are past, but various retail outlets and department stores have leaped in to fill the gap with some pretty elaborate and glossy pre-holiday sales brochures. As a grandfather in his 60s, I find the contents of these modern day "wish books" to be nothing short of amazing. A quick browse through one recent weekend's newspaper Christmas ads yielded some interesting insights into modern life.

Basically, anything that is named after a TV or movie character is a big seller. There are American Gladiator action figures (That's a doll to us old-timers, but don't tell the boys who are playing with them.), Power Ranger figures and equipment, and lots of things bearing the Walt Disney Lion King label.

Come to think of it though, that's nothing new. We had Hopalong Cassidy board games, Lone Ranger cowboy outfits, Shirley Temple dolls, and we read Roy Rogers books. Apparently, the appeal of the media hero or heroine was pretty strong when I was young too.

Toy ads still feature a variety of cars, trucks, police and fire vehicles and construction equipment. If parents are especially generous they can present their child with a remote control toy car for a mere $45.

My brother and I got our share of toy cars and trucks as gifts when we were young. However, none of them were battery-powered. If you wanted them to roll along the floor you pushed them and supplied your own engine sounds as well. One year I did get a real high-tech toy, though. I received a toy bulldozer that was self-propelled by means of a wind up clockwork engine. I'd like to put that baby up against some of these modern battery-powered toys. That wind up caterpillar would climb trees pulling a load if I wanted it to. It, too, was remote controlled - I pointed it in the desired direction, engaged the clutch, and away it went.

One set of items missing from today's new toy ads reflects a sign of the time. There are no farm toys.

Dolls are still very popular, and they come in great numbers and different variety. You can get a doll that does almost anything. I found models that talk, glow in the dark, leave lipstick "kiss prints" on the face of the owner, do gymnastics, whisper, or walk by themselves. For a mere $140 you can buy a model that is about the size of a four-year-old child. This doll's standard costume is a wedding dress large enough to be worn by the child who plays with it. Of course, at the bottom of the page are those boring models that just close their eyes when you lay them down or don't do anything at all. They just feel soft when they're cuddled.

My sister had a modern model that came with a doll baby bottle. When a bottle of water was emptied into the doll's mouth, the water ran out the bottom as if the doll wet its diapers. What a concept. I guess our tastes were simpler then.

Some modern toys are kind of mysterious. There's the toy wood workshop that advertises "cuts wood, not fingers." I want to see that one. My parents just gave me a coping saw. It cut wood, and as long as I kept my fingers out of the way, they didn't get cut. Then, for $20, there's something called Fungeosaurs. I don't think I want anything that sounds like that inside the house.

We always received a certain number of clothing items for Christmas. Often they were things such as new pajamas, shirts, or in my dad's case, sweaters. Clothing is still popular, although styles have changed. Right now a hot outfit consists of faded, baggy jeans, shirts that look wrinkled, leather vests and shoes that look a lot like the ones I wore on the farm. My generation tried like mad to escape wearing things like that - we had worn them for too long. We wanted stuff that was not faded or baggy and didn't look like work boots.

Despite the fact that our toys were pretty low-tech compared to today, the Musfeldt children fared very well at Christmas. As children do today, we reaped a real bounty of gifts. As my brother, sister, and I played with toys and tried on clothes, I occasionally wondered how my dad could look so content with a couple pairs of Rockford socks, a sweater, and bottle of Mennen Skin Bracer. His little pile of gifts looked so small compared to our great blessings. He just sat there with a cup of coffee, watched the rest of us, and smiled.

Apparently some things do stay the same despite changing times and tastes. It was only a few years ago when one of my children said, "Dad has to get into the spirit more. Every year he sits on the couch, drinks coffee, eats cookies, and watches everyone else." I realized something about that time. I didn't feel sorry for Dad anymore. He had all he wanted and so did I.

We Must Have Been Out of Our Minds

The time: Any evening in September, sometime in the '50s
The place: Any 4-H, FFA, or church youth meeting in the Manning area
The question: What shall we do for the October meeting?
The obvious answer: LET'S HAVE A HAY RIDE!

The process: Send out a notice to all members or otherwise advertise the event. Common practice was to write a notice on the front chalkboard in the high school study hall. Next, was a call to some local farmers and implement dealers to secure the donation of two or three hayracks with rubber tires, some bales of straw (Alfalfa was a lousy substitute despite the name "hay ride."), and the use of farm tractors to pull the hayracks. Pretty much any tractors would suffice as long as they were equipped with headlights and rubber tires. Sound strange? More than a few farm tractors in use during the mid-50s were not equipped with headlights and a few still rolled through the fields on steel, lug-equipped wheels. Such models were not good hay ride material. Tail lights or rear reflectors on the hayracks were optional, since the state of Iowa didn't require such equipment or slow moving symbols until later. Finally, recruit two or three semi-sane farm boys to drive the tractors. After that, just pray for a pleasantly brisk, clear fall night.

◆ ◆ ◆

A mellow harvest moon rises over the hills east of town. The crisp tang of fall is in the air. It's not too warm and not too cool. Laughter and greetings fill the air as the passengers pick their chosen chariots. Usually, one went for the front rig since each succeeding rack was dustier and subject to straw barrages from the rack in front. Lots of attention was given to which rack was picked by certain members of opposite gender so later activities might be arranged. The leader makes the usual speech - "Don't open the bales until we're out of town. Don't throw straw at cars. Don't throw straw at one another. Stay on the racks. No necking." Well, it all sounded good. What a pleasant, peaceful, rural evening...

    The semi-sane farm boys kicked the snarling tractor engines into life. Hayrack passengers were stacked up like cordwood against the back of the rack as the tractor jockeys slammed the transmissions into road gear, and the whole caravan roared off at full throttle. With any luck the tractors were Farmalls or early model John Deeres with the two range transmissions. Those babies would *roll!* Fifteen miles per hour seemed like 50 at night. The first straw bales were broken open within a block and a half. The first wad of straw hit an oncoming car within the next block and a half. Some fool had already jumped off the last rack and was racing like a madman toward the front rack with a double handful of straw. He hung in there for a few yards, and then some friends on the last rack grabbed arms and coat collar and drug him aboard lest he get left in the dust. If anyone thought the driver would slow down and let them back on in such circumstances, they were sadly mistaken.
    Flashing lights now bring the procession to a halt. It seems the first car bombarded with straw was the Manning police car. (True story.) The little green Studebaker Lark with the spotlight on the side

was gaily decorated with straw from one end to the other. "Shorty" Ehlers had a limited sense of humor. A few "Yes, sir's" and "We won't do it any more" and we're on the road again.

*I guess it never occurred to us that danger might be involved in this process. Only years later, while setting out on a similar event with my college sophomore class did I realize there was another point of view. I believe the city-bred class president's words were something like, "**Are you nuts?! Somebody could get hurt if they fell off at this speed! Find a lower gear!**" He was kind of pale and shaky at that point. He later questioned what anyone could expect from farm guys who drove their cars 70 miles an hour down gravel roads.*

The semi-sane farm boys throttled down a bit, and the hayracks basked in the glow of the harvest moon. Discreetly, the tractors' rear-facing implement lights were turned off or covered. The shouting and laughter tapered to mellow conversation, and a few passengers were blissfully disobeying the leader's final rule.

The caravan came to the end of the ride. Passengers shook the straw out of their hair and clothing. Tractors purred at a satisfied idle. Leaders and chaperones breathed sighs of thanks and relief. There was a chorus of "goodbye" and "see-you-later," and many smiles at the thought of repeating the great event again next year!

A New Little World

The slew or "slough" if you prefer, on the north side of the road is a distant memory. It must not have made much of an impression early in my life. Once, when Dad and Uncle Hank went pheasant hunting along its edge, a big flock of pheasants exploded from among the dry horseweed canes. They just kept coming in two's, three's, and four's until it seemed that they numbered in the hundreds. That's about all I remember about the slew......until they "tiled it out."

It was probably the two little Army surplus Jeeps, one with that intriguing machine mounted on the back that got my attention as they pulled into the field driveway that morning. The Jeep with the trencher was positioned on one end of the slew and the other Jeep was on the opposite end. A cable was then extended from a winch on the front of the trencher Jeep to the rear bumper hitch on the other. As its little engine roared, the trencher Jeep dropped the digging tool into the ground and began to inch across the slew by the slow and steady operation of the winch. In its wake it left a neat, three-foot-deep by eight-inch-wide ditch flanked by two long mounds of slimy, black mud. At the bottom of that trench they laid a line of round, brick colored tile.

As a curious nine-year-old, I got Dad's permission to accompany him for a closer look at the work in progress. Following the trail left by the trenching machine into the thicket of willows and horseweeds, I really met the slew for the first time.

It was a great surprise.

What was revealed was a three acre, partially wooded swamp. Clear pools like tiny lakes were joined by narrow creeks into a maze of waterways. Willow bushes overhung the pools, and shiny green frogs hopped and paddled to escape the oncoming invaders. I remember the sense of delight in discovering a new little world.

Underlying the horseweeds, willows, and pools of water was a several-foot-deep layer of black porous soil, which, when mixed with water by the machines, became a bottomless, black ooze of cake batter consistency. The trenching Jeep became bogged down so thoroughly at one point that the other Jeep had to be replaced with a heavy farm tractor, since the winch simply drug the anchor Jeep backwards into the slew instead of moving the trencher through the mud.

In a couple of days the two Jeeps headed back to Halbur, dripping and muddy. Their task was finished – and so was the slew. My new-found world had come to an end.

For some months, the newly implanted drainage system poured a solid stream of cold, clear water from its eight-inch galvanized throat. The little lakes dried up, the frogs died or moved downstream, and the area assumed the appearance of a very shaggy, untidy, and somewhat battered weed patch. Later, the willows were bulldozed and burned, and the following spring, my first-ever field task on a tractor was to help turn the slew into a productive field which it remains to this day.

I don't know how often this scenario was repeated in the Manning area during that time, but I do know it was common. In fact, the later discovery of a similar tile outlet revealed that a downstream pasture on our farm had also been tiled out decades before, as had many other wetlands or "bottoms" in the surrounding countryside.

I don't wish to over-romanticize the whole event, nor do I presume to pass judgment on the generations of Iowa farmers who drained those wetland areas for farm land. After all, I don't have to try to make a living and feed a family from that soil; they did.

I do, however, sometimes wonder if, in the reflective words of a retired Manning farmer who is now deceased, "we outsmarted ourselves" by draining all those slews. Did the removal of those natural upstream water filters contribute to the appearance of dozens of polluted wells with the eventual need for a costly rural water system? Did the disabling of that slowdown system contribute to increased soil erosion as those little streams now roared full with brown, silty water after every heavy rain, as the tilled field could not slow the runoff? Did the value of the crops produced on that land exceed the cost of losing the wetlands?

I don't know the answer. Does anyone?

There are few of those upland slews left in the Manning area. There is probably less clear creek water and fewer frogs, horseweeds and willows. I'm not sure if it's even important whether there are or not...

But sometimes, in a nostalgic moment, I sort of wish some farmer, who could afford to do so, would plug up the tile and let the whole works sit for a couple of years and see what would happen...

It would be interesting to see what kind of new little world might emerge.

Not Lately

Our house has a large yard. Not five acres or anything like that, but large for a suburban yard. Like all backyards, it produces a certain quantity of trash and trimmings which must occasionally be moved around. So...I own a pitchfork.

It's not fancy or new; I bought it at a garage sale, I think. It's not a collector's item, but it is sort of unique: it has four tines. Yes, it is a real pitchfork with four tines instead of the usual three. It's nothing real special – just a four tine pitchfork – but, it's a nice pitchfork – it works – and I use it every so often.

While turning over the contents of my compost bin, I broke the handle on my pitchfork. It must have been cracked already, since I'm not all that muscular. I thought to myself, "I'll have to go get a new handle."

You bet...

If TV football commentator, John Madden, really wants to hand his "Ace Hardware Man" a challenge, let him ask for a pitchfork handle. In the words of the late comedian George Gobel, "You can't hardly get those kind anymore."

The first response to such a request is usually, "Pitchfork..?" Often followed by, "We don't carry handles, but we have four-tine yard forks, they're only $21.95."

No thanks, I've seen those new chain store forks. We did better metal work than that in Mr. Laverty's industrial arts shop at MHS.

"If you find a handle, it'll probably cost as much as a new fork."

I'll take my chances.

Well, three places carried them. The prices ranged from $12.95 at one True Value Hardware to $7.95 at a thrift store.

My fork now has a new handle...it's happy...the thrift store man is happy...my compost bin is happy...and I'm happy.

After spending about half a day on this little project, I began to feel a bit out of date, or at least out of touch. I guess people just don't put new handles on pitchforks anymore. They probably don't even have pitchforks. Pitchforks date back to an era when people pitched things: things like loose hay and oats bundles at threshing time. That was a while back though. Lots of modern people know the term, but probably have never seen one.

I wonder what my hardware man would have done if I'd given him some real tough ones like:
- a hay knife (No, I don't think the Swiss Army used them.)
- a chicken hook, or
- cow hobbles.

It's amazing how a word, phrase, or object which is so commonly mentioned and understood in one decade can sound so oddly old-fashioned to the same ears only a seeming few years later. Here a few more items from the old "I haven't thought of those in years" file.
- bullet pencils
- store string
- summer kitchens
- section cars
- gypsy wagons
- milk pails
- window weights

I wonder if 50 years from now anyone will mention lawn mowers, VCRs, CDs, or Air Jordans. Time will tell.

Watch Your Fingers

My father pulled the tractor and mounted corn picker into the yard and turned off the engine. It was still light, and it was uncharacteristic of him to come in early from the field. Walking into the house, he laid his leather gloves on the kitchen table. With scarcely a word he pointed to the middle finger of the right hand glove. The end of the glove finger had been clipped off as cleanly as if by a razor – a hair's breadth beyond the end of his finger. He never saw or felt it happen. "What bothers me is I don't even know where I did it," was his only comment.

Dad spent some time in the seat of the silent machine examining it for likely places to lose a finger. After some time he felt he had the answer. The Case picker had a device called a stalk extractor. Two spinning ribbed metal rollers grabbed loose cornstalks before they reached the elevator and spit them out a curved metal chute. The ribs on the rollers and the leading edge of the sheet metal chute formed perfect shears, strong and sharp enough to easily cut leather - or flesh and bone of any fingers reaching to clear a stubborn stalk.

Thus the stories went each fall when the beginning of the corn harvest brought tales of tragedy and warning in newspapers and on farm radio programs. "Be very careful when operating a corn picker!"

The mechanical corn picker put the American Corn Belt into overdrive. Farmers could plant and harvest more acres quickly and cleanly with much less manual labor. A farmer and one son, wife, or hired man could do the work of five hand picking laborers. Higher yields of hybrid corn filled corn cribs and wire mesh rings to overflowing. More grain went to feed more livestock and family farming changed scale forever.

But...

The mechanical corn picker, especially the tractor mounted variety, had another side. This labor saving blessing had more frightful hazards per square bolt than any farm machine seen before. Clawing gathering chains and snapping rollers reached for the careless and unwary. Spinning sprockets and bicycle chains could grab a loose sleeve or glove in an instant. Power take off shafts, spun at more than 500 revolutions per minute by the big tractor engine, could wind up 13 feet of rope a second...much less a three-foot pant leg. And then there was the husking bed – a series of metal and rubber rollers lying side by side. The spinning rollers tore the husks from the ears of corn in milliseconds, just within reach of any careless hand brushing away debris.

Despite warnings from radio and press, and having heard the horror stories from men who no longer had one hand, farm workers did become careless. Worse still, some farmers removed important safety shields in order to "get at" moving parts for repair or adjustments. The consequences were always hazardous and sometimes tragic.

On a fall visit to Manning, I watched a local farmer harvesting corn with a combine. Seeing the operator riding high in safety and comfort in the combine cab, I had to reflect on the changes in mechanical farming. Remembering the crisp tang of those fall days with that peculiar buzzing rumble of corn pickers to be heard in various neighbors' fields and the steady stream of ear-corn laden wagons flowing into corn cribs, I recall a sense of bounty and fulfillment. But those days also had their dark side, and the safe completion of corn picking season was always reason for rejoicing.

Guys, I don't know where the hazards are on those big combines, but keep your hands out of places they don't belong, and have a bumper crop!

We Had One

During the time of the Manning Centennial, a friend happily observed that the number of antique tractors in the Centennial parade had been limited, since for city residents they weren't necessarily an item of great and immediate interest. In giving the comment some thought, I had to agree. To those living in town a tractor is just a tractor; on the other hand, to a great number of farm boys, the tractor was the ultimate symbol of rural life and lifestyle in the exploding mechanical age of the mid-20th century.

Some people knew real estate, some people knew cars, and we farm boys knew tractors. They were at the very center of our existence. As kids we watched our elders operate those fascinating machines. At country school recess the conversation (or arguments) often centered around the subject of tractors. Which brand was best? What was new on the market? Could an Allis out-pull a Case? Was a Farmall faster than a John Deere?

We knew all the makes, the models, the engines, and the features. We knew that Massey Harris tractors were red, Fergusons were gray, and Olivers were green. Any farm kid worth his salt could tell the difference between a John Deere model A and a model B blindfolded. We could tell the brand and model of many tractors just by hearing the sound of the engine. A trip with Dad to Albert Puck's, Herman Frahm's, or Tom Knudsen's implement companies was sheer pleasure as we climbed aboard the new John Deere, Case or Farmall tractors. We sniffed the aroma of new paint and rubber and fantasized what it would be like to drive one. Power steering, torque amplifiers, and live hydraulics were new gadgets, and the delivery of a new tractor to the farm was met with the excitement that a new car generates for us now.

The most significant rite of passage for many of us was that time when our farmer fathers stepped away from the tractor for the first time, tried to look confident and uttered those timeless words,

"Don't turn too short on the ends, and leave it in second gear. That's fast enough." That first solo tour around the field with the future of a year's crop and several thousand pounds of roaring power in our youthful hands is a trip remembered by every farm kid who ever hooked a harrow cable with a rear tire or sprained a whole set of fingers on a kicking back steering wheel.

The tractor was the focus of what being a grown up farmer was all about, and we who experienced those times, regardless of our current life situations, will never forget that special relationship we had with the farm tractor.

In a secluded corner of the Oregon State Fair near the end of the horse barn stands a quiet exhibit. The restored antique farm tractors stand in groups and rows, painted and polished to look just like new. Most of the large crowds and particularly young people from the city give the gleaming giants only passing attention, if any at all. But if you stand and watch for a while, you can see people in ones and twos quietly and carefully examining each detail of the restored tractors as if to make sure that no part was neglected by the restorer. And every so often, perhaps from a long urbanized farm boy, the quiet, almost loving tribute to the silent machine, "We had one just like that."

Let's See What You're Made Of
Heritage Part I

Over the years, I've read with interest *Manning Monitor* coverage of the Weihnachtsfest celebration. It's great to see Manning enjoying and celebrating its German heritage. Its special events and decorations certainly contribute to a joyous holiday. The German emphasis of Weihnachtsfest and the establishment of the Hausbarn Heritage Park celebrate the roots of many local customs and the cultural heritage of many Manning residents.

The largest part of a person's or a community's heritage, however, cannot be captured in print or reproduced in a festival. It cannot be put on display, sung or tasted. The essence of our heritage is within us. Our heritage is, to a great extent, who we are. We are born a child of our parents, and as we grow, we are shaped by the persons and events around us.

Weihnachtsfest brought special lighting to Main Street, outlining buildings with hundreds of white lights, but beautiful Christmas lights are also part of the seasons of beauty in Manning's past. This community has traditionally taken on a festive look during the holidays and one of the highlights of the season has been viewing the Christmas display at Ohde Funeral Home. How many carloads of people have driven by to view the Ohde decorations over the years?

Another holiday observance of my youth was lining up in front of the Virginia Café to receive a stocking filled with candy and fruit from Santa Claus (who, despite the mask and all, sounded a lot like Pete Kuhl). I never quite figured out why Santa left his sleigh at home for a ride in the back of one of Ramsey's trucks, but it didn't really matter.

The heritage within us is what prompts Manning grocers to lay in a stock of oysters at this time of year and the Manning Pharmacy to carry anise oil. There may never be an oyster stew stand or a Peppernut booth during Weihnachtsfest, but for many, those were and still are Christmas staples.

Would music and carol singing have the same meaning without Manning's religious heritage? Whether German or not, Lutheran, Catholic, Methodist, Presbyterian, or Baptist; Manning residents grew up with church Christmas programs and services. It's appropriate that local churches are involved in Weihnachtsfest, since religious activities have always played such a strong part in Manning's history.

More and more I realize that my own personal Christmas heritage is a grand aggregate of rural school Christmas programs, grit voos, Lutheran Christianity, oyster stew, Bing Crosby, snowy rural roads, roast goose at Uncle Herman's, toys displayed at the dime store, packing eggs in the basement while Santa came and a host of other experiences.

Weihnachtsfest is a special festival, but it's not special because it's German, or ambitious, or famous, or any other such reason. It's special because it's a celebration of who you are, what you've become, and how you got there. May Manning residents continue to celebrate the heritage of their hearts and mold all those who follow.

To Each His Own
Heritage Part II

Each year, Manning residents take part in a tree planting project. Homeowners are encouraged to plant young trees and to nurture them with care and "one five-gallon bucket of water per week." Bingo. Heritage.

People in cities rarely water their plants with five-gallon buckets; people in rural areas do that. City dwellers measure water in minutes and inches, usually not in five-gallon buckets.

This is not meant to make fun of a local expression, but rather to point out that heritage shows itself in odd ways and at unexpected times. To each his own.

Those five-gallon buckets are now found stacked in the entry area of a large home improvement and hardware chain. Years ago, those pails were often the left over container of some used up commodity. Rural Iowans, being very practical, used the container for another purpose instead of simply throwing it away. Lots of things used to come packaged in five-gallon buckets, hence a unit of measure that everyone in the area understands and uses regularly.

Heritage is all around us. It's the way we dress, the way we talk, the things we do for recreation, and the way we view the world.

Manning area farmers have on occasion banded together to plant or harvest crops for an injured or ailing neighbor. In 1956, neighbors helped Henry Sonksen rebuild a barn that blew down in that year's storm. That's heritage – a sense of community that shows itself in helping others.

Please forgive a bit of nostalgia and then make up your own list. Heritage is:
- Noon whistles blowing from the water tower
- Eating Grit Voos as though everyone did it
- Pheasant hunting in November
- Driving around town on a warm summer evening
- Waving to people on porches and in cars, even when you're not quite sure who it is
- Dried beef sandwiches in the summer
- Brick streets
- Still hearing a word or two of German in a conversation
- Grandpa's shotgun
- Basketball games
- Striped coveralls
- Children's Day
- Softball games on Sunday afternoon
- Family reunions in the park

Make up your own list. Everyone's is different.

A few years ago I visited a home in Palo Alto, California. In the midst of this sophisticated, wealthy, educated city lived a family of former Iowans. In their house they kept a few antiques that reminded them of "home." Among the usual bottles and pictures in this fine home, up on the wall in a place of honor rested the centerpiece – the ultimate symbol of their growing up in Iowa - a chicken hook! ... To each his own.

Back in the Grove

Back in the grove was a mystical place
The air had a different smell;
The odor of seasons of leaves that decayed
And then joined with the soil where they fell.

The bird songs had kind of an echo-y sound
That would ring through the air like a chime;
And the red squirrel barked at intruders who came,
While the woodpecker's tapping kept time.

There were green ash, and walnut, and box elder too,
With a tiny creek wandering by.
And the leaves and the branches spread shade over all,
Growing so close they shut out the sky.

On the edge of the cool, shady grove one could find
Wild strawberries ripe every spring.
And the prickly vines that would scratch at the touch
Yielded raspberries, tiny, but fine.

The hollowed-out maple where raccoons had lived
Leaned over, was perfect to climb.
And the mulberries, tasty for people and birds
Were a curse to Mom's clothes on the line.

There were treasures just waiting to be found as well,
As imaginations ran free.
A piece of horse harness, a nail, or a bone;
What's their story; what caused them to be?

The old pistol, rusted, and partially gone
Told no tales, but woke wonderful dreams.
It was said that the Gypsies once camped 'neath these trees.
Maybe outlaws planned out evil schemes.

Pieces of rusted old farm implements
That had found here their final reward
Became airplanes and rocket ships soaring away,
Or a tank charging off into war.

Small saplings worked fine for the ceiling and walls
Of the play houses built with such pride,
And the low growing fork of the box elder tree
Was a saddle on horseback to ride.

As the seasons marched by with the leaves come and gone,
There was always a new sight to see,
And my regular "field trips" back into the grove
Were always a pleasure to me.

There are lots of fine places I've been in my time
That have brought peace and rest to my soul,
But on some hard days I'd give half a month's pay
For one childhood hour back in the grove.

If Mupps Was Here...

It's going to be an early spring in the northwest. The signs are all there: early budding of trees, warmer temperatures and 'possums on the move. That's right, yesterday morning I looked out the window and saw the first 'possum of spring waddling across the backyard.

'Possums. Now there's a subject for an article all by itself. But it wasn't just the oddities of 'possums that came to mind as I looked out the window. The first thought was, "If only Mupps were here. That 'possum's days would be numbered." Some things just never quite disappear from memory. Mupps is one of those things.

Nothing special about Mupps. She was an average looking black and white border collie. She never had a lot of grooming. Never ate a lot of special food, unless you count the baby pig pellets she'd snack on in the feed shed. She refused to sleep anywhere but on the front porch even in severe weather. In snowy weather she would lie down in the middle of the front lawn and let the snow cover her up. When Dad came out the kitchen door to do the morning chores, a little mound of snow would explode into an enthusiastic farm dog ready to head for work. A couple of rolls in the snow for good measure and she'd head for the farmyard and a new day.

Mupps was just a farm dog. One of many. They came in all sizes, breeds and shapes. Hib Eischeid's Shep was a big, gold collie/shepherd. Uncle Albert's Dobbin, another shepherd, was good with cattle. Hank Sonksen's feisty little rat terrier, Pooch, could hold her own with the best. They were just farm dogs, but you can bet when conversation flowed around the corn sheller at coffee time, at least part of that conversation would touch on the latest feats of those constant farmers' companions, the farm dogs.

These were not the pampered pooches of dog shows or the family pet that slept on the living room rug. These were working dogs. Oh, they liked to be petted and played with, but when Dad or one of the boys headed for the barn, it was back to business. They worked for their keep. When Mom went out to feed the chickens, the dog went along. When Dad went to feed cattle or headed out to plow, the dog went along. When the kids went to get the cows for milking, the dog went along. When a 'possum or 'coon invaded the chicken house, the dog was there. If strange noises came from the cattle or hog yard during the night, the dog checked it out. We never left our yard light on at night. If someone decided to make a stealthy entry onto the Musfeldt or Eischeid farm places at night, they would have to get past Mupps or Shep. Take my word; it wouldn't have been a pleasant task.

The qualifications for a good farm dog were rigid. There was no compromise. No playful chasing of livestock, at home or anywhere else. Be ready to take on any raccoon, 'possum, badger, or prowler that threatens the safety or welfare of the farm or the family. Be patient with the kids and wary of anyone who is unknown. No biting without reason. Be willing to sleep, work, and eat under less than ideal circumstances in all kinds of weather. Stay at home and not roam the countryside at night. Violations of these rules would bring a reprimand. Livestock chasing, biting children and roaming were serious offenses. They could bring the death penalty. There was kind of an unwritten code that shooting any roaming dog found near livestock was not a crime.

The farm dog belonged to the farm, or the farm to it. Who owned who was always in question. When Mom and Dad moved to town, Mupps stayed on the farm with its new tenant, Eddie Sextro. He may have bought the place and lived there, but the farm belonged to Mupps. There was no doubt about it.

It Must Be About Time

It must be about time for the thresher's meeting... The oats are ripe and ready to cut. Most of the fellows in the threshing (pronounced "thrashing") ring have pulled out the binders, checked over the canvasses, picked up a bundle of twine and perhaps taken the sickle in to 'Hannes Bunz for sharpening. Some have already begun the first step in the process - cutting the oats during the hot part of the day and then in the cool of the morning and evening, stacking the twine-tied bundles into neat, symmetrical, six- or eight-bundle shocks...

Threshing was kind of an "in-between" process. Between the time when man harvested the grain for daily bread by beating it from the stalks with a flail or treading it out beneath the hooves of animals, and the time when huge, diesel-powered combines wipe the grain from the fields in one great sweep, there was threshing.

Grain was cut and tied into neat bundles by a binder, shocked for curing, and then hauled to that huge, humming machine to be separated from the straw. Threshing took lots of man, woman, and child hours to accomplish.

Of all farming tasks, I think mechanical progress made the most dramatic change to the labor that was involved with small grain harvesting. It took two people to operate a tractor-drawn binder (one if it was horse-drawn), one or more men to shock the bundles of grain, and a crew of dozens for the actual threshing task. There were bundle pitchers, tractor drivers, oats haulers, cooks, dish washers and sometimes, straw stackers. Heading up the whole works was the engineer.

...Some of the guys have already dropped out of the threshing ring and bought combines. Fewer farmers and smaller families with fewer boys to work the farm have begun to take their toll. There will be five farms in the ring this year instead of eight. That means we'll have to hire some spike pitchers from town or maybe some neighborhood farmers. It's tough to find people who will do that hard work, and every hired man brings up the cost per bushel...

It was hard work. For that two-week period the farmers did their own chores early, and then spent the day pitching bundles, sometimes several miles away from the home place. At home, Mom and the kids took care of watering livestock in the hot weather. They would start the evening chores which Dad finished up after dark before falling into bed for a short, hot, night's sleep. When the crew was at their farm, the farmer's wife was responsible for supplying the workers with morning lunch, dinner at noon, afternoon lunch, and cool water in between.

...It will probably be hot again this year. How come oats always have to get ripe during the hottest part of the summer? It will be 90 degrees in the shade and humid. We'll work and sweat in that itchy oats dust or (God forbid) those barley beards that stick to sweaty skin and crawl around inside of clothes where the chiggers also love to roam...

I guess we didn't know any better. We just complained a little and kept on working. Only once did Hib shut 'er down on a hot day, and that had more to do with how the dry grain was threshing than creature comfort. A couple of minutes in the shade of a hayrack, a long drink of water from the common dipper hanging on the cream can, and it was back to the field we went.

We just sort of stuck together until it was done. Threshing rings were one of the last real exercises in mutual dependency for the Midwest farmer. When the last drive belt was rolled up and the last Case, Twin Cities, or Red River Special threshing machine was parked out behind the last grove, American farming changed forever. Certainly people still work together and help one another, but never again will that exercise of joyfully sharing the labor in completing the harvest task be carried out on such a scale.

...Yup, Dad says the thresher's meeting is Thursday. That means we'll be starting in a week or so. It's really fun, you know, all getting together with the tractors, racks, and pickups. Maybe next year we'll get a combine, too, but this year will still be exciting. I wonder who'll tip the first load of bundles and have to buy the first case...

The Great Window Painting Contest

The tension was so thick you could have cut it with a knife! Anxious eyes looked for any sign of approval on the faces of the judges. The task was finished; the verdict now rested solely in the hands of that small group of people whose mission it was to determine the winner of the Great Halloween Window painting contest.

It was a noble idea. The Manning Main Street merchants had decreed a Halloween window painting contest. Whether the idea originated as publicity, public service, support of area rural schools, or as a ploy to divert Halloween artistic urges in a controlled direction rather than in the direction of neighborhood auto windshields is not fully known.

Whatever the motivation, one fine October, Manning area rural schools were invited to select their best artists and enter them in a window painting contest to be held on Main Street. Each participating school would be assigned a store front window donated by a merchant, issued a supply of tempera paint, and encouraged to render a painting based on a Halloween theme.

And so the schools selected their most capable artists. Teachers and pupils put artistic energy to the task of deciding upon just the right picture for their glass canvas. Even sample drawings were done and refinements made. At last, all were prepared for the tournament.

Painting day dawned gray, nasty, and bitter cold. Frigid fingers fumbled with paintbrushes dipped in an icy approximation of tempera paint. Nervous artists, parents, and friends walked from group to group evaluating the competition. Teacher Irma Bromert provided moral support and hot chocolate obtained at a nearby restaurant to four junior high aged boys who had been selected as artists on the basis of pictures confiscated during arithmetic class. Artistic juices flowed and excitement reigned.

Finally the allotted time had expired, and it was time for the judging. A hush fell over each section of sidewalk as the little group of judges moved with dignity from window to window. The creative labor of enthusiastic hands was carefully viewed from various angles to get the full impact. Who would win – the witch and pumpkin, the corn shock and jack-o-lantern, or the mural of the headless horseman?

One picture was finally awarded first place, but there were no losers. Main Street never looked more festive, enthusiasm and community spirit was never higher, and no Halloween will ever pass for some of us without recalling that frigid October day when we were part of the Great Window Painting Contest.

A Word of Thanks

What elementary school student hasn't received one of those writing assignments designed to help them reflect on life's experiences? "What I did during summer vacation." "What I would like for Christmas." "Things I am thankful for."

I don't know how many papers I've written on the subject of Thanksgiving, but there have been a few. I suppose those I wrote as a child reflected a child's view of things - "I'm thankful for my dog, my mother and father, my new BB gun, my new Sunday clothes and Thanksgiving dinner." Fair enough. Those things were all important to a school boy. But different ages bring different perspectives. It might have been interesting to have had our parents write a similar paper:

Things I'm Thankful For
Rural Iowa, Mid-20th Century

First of all, I'm thankful for a crop. That's how it is with farming; you buy the gas, invest in seed, put in a lot of work, and then you wait, and watch, and "if." You know, "if" we get enough rain for crops to grow but not so much that everything washes out, "if" the corn borers aren't too bad this year, "if" we don't get a bad hail storm, or wind storm, or dry spell, or...

I'm thankful there are oats in the bin, there's corn in the crib, there's hay and straw in the barn, and there's water in the well. Our livestock should make it through the winter all right. Just so we have enough to feed out the cattle and hogs next summer, and we don't have to sell before they're at market weight.

I'm thankful everyone's healthy. Farming is a hazardous occupation. Between operating machinery, backbreaking work in hot weather, livestock handling, and just the day to day business of making a living from the tilling of soil, there are lots of places accidents can happen. Measles, Whooping Cough, Polio, and Scarlet Fever are becoming less common, and we worry less about the kids.

I'm thankful we managed to get a good teacher for our rural school. More schools close each year, and it's getting harder and harder to get teachers willing to deal with the distance and isolation of teaching in "country school." I'm thankful the loans for last season are paid off. We have some extra cash now to buy new clothes. We'll have enough for heating oil during the winter, and it should be a good Christmas.

I'm thankful none of our local boys are fighting in a war right now. We hoped that after *The War*, we wouldn't be sending boys off again for a long time. But, then, before we knew it, everything started up again in Korea. Thank God that's over, and we pray it will be a long time before another one.

That was another time and I was another age - weren't we all? It was a different kind of rural America with a different set of needs, worries, and joys. However, the basics still seem to remain the same when you get right down to it. We're still linked to family, health, security, and peace.

I expect that teachers still occasionally ask the question, "What are you thankful for?" I also expect that baby brothers or sisters, puppies, new bikes, pretty fall leaves, and Thanksgiving dinner are still popular answers. Perhaps an enterprising teacher of adults might even give the same assignment to their students. It's never too late, and we're never too old, to count and share the blessings of our lives.

Picture Perfect

It didn't always snow before Christmas. Some years the frozen ground was almost entirely bare. No wind-packed drifts blocked the house yard gate. No frozen glaze coated the roads. No mounds of white bent tree branches.

Why is it then, that my clearest Christmas memory involves snow? It's a mental motion picture of dry, fluffy flakes floating down in the glow of the single-bulb yard light. I can feel the tingle of cold on my cheeks and hear the crunch of snow beneath my buckle overshoes. It's dark, and I'm on my way back to the house after finishing some late evening farm chore. The yellowish glow from the farm house windows promises warmth, comfort, and supper.

That little moment-in-time memory could probably apply to any one of a hundred winter evenings in my youth. Why does my memory insist on linking it with Christmas?

Perhaps it's because Christmas is such a small memory. Oh, yes there's a great hub-bub made of the whole thing. Even years back, things kind of picked up speed in December. School kids made gifts, memorized recitations, and learned songs in preparation for the Christmas program. Grocery stores took on that distinctive aroma as crates of oranges and grapefruit perfumed the air. Rows of Christmas trees leaned against the front of the Council Oak and Darrell Bales' Market. Al Martens and Ed Knaack packed the shelves of the Ben Franklin store with extra quantities of toys, and Herman Pahde brought in some pretty new holiday dresses. Sunday School children rehearsed the story of Baby Jesus in the manger. Mothers and fathers made the best use of school days and midnight oil, hiding gifts and making preparations out of the sight of curious, youthful eyes. Much action and excitement were evident.

But, when you get right down to it, much of Christmas centered around really small things. For all the running back and forth, the whole focus of the holiday kind of narrows. Christmas in my memory is not huge and cosmic and all that. It's our family gathered in that century-old farmhouse. The world sort of began and ended with those walls that evening. Sure, we went to church services and school programs, and those were great and meaningful events. Absolutely, holiday family gatherings with oyster stew, roast goose, and all those wonderful trimmings were fun and festive; but the heart and core of the holiday still was our family in that farmhouse.

As Christmas approached each year, the progression of events marked the passing of the days. The arrival of the Montgomery Ward Christmas catalog, Christmas decorations appearing in the stores, exciting smells from the kitchen – each day brought a new reminder: Christmas was coming.

The final sign that things were on the home stretch at the Musfeldt household was the appearance of the bells in the dining room window. When my sister, brother, and I arrived home from school to see that festive arrangement of bows, beads, and bells, we knew that the Christmas season had truly arrived.

Memory - what a magical gift. It allows us to put all those things together into the perfect mental picture – maybe even more ideal than it really was – but perfect, nonetheless.

The snowflakes drift lazily down past the yard light. It's dark, and I can feel the crunch of snow beneath my buckle overshoes as I head back to the house, drawn by that yellowish light that means warmth and comfort – and guided by the bells in the window.

Now That Was a Winter

The late television personality Johnny Carson got a lot of mileage throughout his career with his "How cold was it?" gags, but his list would pale in comparison to the list one might build with an Iowa winter "How bad was it?" contest. Nearly every Iowan has at least one story to tell about that awful winter when…

If you want some real beauties, you need to gather a few former Iowans who now live in less severe climates. If one were to believe all the tales told by these ex-patriots, every winter recorded at least one 50-degree below zero night, all children lived ten miles from school on impassable roads, and burrowing through 20-foot-high snow drifts to get to the barn at milking time was routine.

Most of these grand stories originate in a rural context, perhaps because nowhere in modern society can a major blizzard or prolonged cold snap pose more problems, challenges, or even danger than on an Iowa farm. For those of us raised on farms in the '40s and '50s, being snowed in was not an unusual event. Some severe winters produced repeated bouts with closed roads and drifts that had to finally be moved with a bulldozer after the regular snow plows could no longer handle the bulk of packed snow.

Candles and kerosene or white gas lamps were real necessities. More than once our farm house weathered a severe blizzard in the glow of flickering flames because the power was out. Those evenings spent quietly around our wood and coal dining room heating stove, with the sound of crackling fire and the rustle of my parents' newspapers playing calm counterpoint to the whirling winds and the shudder of storm windows, provide some of the most vivid memories of my childhood.

Chuck Offenburger, the *Des Moines Register's* "Iowa Boy" wrote that "You know you're in a small town when after a major snowstorm, the farmers all have a race to see who can be the first one to get to town, sit in the coffee shop and talk about how tough it was to get to town." I don't know about the race part, but at one time this drama would have been acted out in Manning fashion at Emil Kuhl's Highway Café. Housed in what was more recently the Hawkeye Diesel service building adjacent to Puck Implement. Emil's little café was a real men's gathering place. On a cold winter morning it was a collage of ear flaps, steamed-over windows, coveralls, five buckle overshoes, melted snow puddles, cigarette smoke, hot pork sandwiches, coffee, laughter, and storm stories. A boy could learn something about the world of men here over a cup of hot chocolate.

As the stories of stuck equipment, endangered livestock, and record snow drifts spun around the room, a subtle undercurrent flowed through the conversations. Beyond the tales of hardship, heroism, and even humor, there emerged a sense of common need and mutual support. These men all faced a common enemy, a brutal Midwest winter storm. If one listened closely, between the lines the message came through, "We're okay. We made it through another one. We passed the test – together."

They Did it All
Rural Schools I

The days were beginning to grow shorter. The oats had been threshed and the second cutting of clover was in the barn. Locusts filled the evenings with a penetrating buzz and blackbirds were gathering in large flocks, preparing for the trip south. It was then that the director of the local rural school board loaded up his tools and headed for the schoolyard. The summer had produced a bumper crop of tall grass and weeds on the unused playground. A tractor and a six-foot sickle mower would take care of that problem. The gallon can of gasoline was set in a handy place as a remedy for the inevitable nest of bumblebees who had taken up residence in a depression in the ground.

The five-gallon cans of water, broom, and soap would spruce up the idle outhouses while a sharp eye was kept for any wasp nests that may have been constructed under the eaves during the summer. A saw came in handy for trimming storm damaged trees around the perimeter of the schoolyard. A hammer and a few 12-penny nails took care of any loose boards in the fence. After a quick survey to see that no windows had been broken by vandals and that no raccoons or 'possums had moved in through an unlocked basement door or window, only an inspection of the swing chains, turning bar, and the sandbox remained. A return trip in a few days to rake up the mown grass and collected tree branches would ready the outside of the building for the beginning of school. One adjustment to the scheduled tasks was called for. A pocket gopher had left a trail of mounds across the playground. The director's son (or daughter) would be sent over with a steel gopher trap to eliminate the culprit.

While the director had been preparing the school grounds, a group of school mothers was turning their attention to the interior of the building. After a good sweeping, the dry wood floor was given a generous coat of floor oil as a preservative and for the sake of appearance. There were few waxed or varnished floors in these utilitarian buildings. The cobwebs were swept out of the corners and the windows cleaned inside and out. Library shelves were dusted, school desks washed, and the slate blackboards were washed to an ebony shine.

School board directors in the rural school districts of Iowa weren't mere figureheads; nor were they order-givers or simply complaint listeners - they did it all. From convening School Board meetings to purchasing equipment to cleaning the outhouses, the school board director was responsible for the school. This was citizen participation "up close and personal." The task did not always fall on the same man. (It was always a man.) The job was rotated through the ranks of school parents so the work got spread around a bit. The job did run in families, however. Clifford Tank served as director of the same school as his father before him.

There was true parent participation in the school. Teachers were chosen by the school board composed of parents. Parents built the swings, mowed the grass, checked out the furnace and ordered the load of coal for the winter. (These responsibilities did not usually extend to starting the fire on winter mornings; the teacher did that.) If school was going to happen, the school board and the parents would have to make it happen - there were no paid district employees to step in and fill the gaps.

A classic example occurred at the school on Henry Sonksen's corner (now Leroy Albertson's corner, one mile east and four miles north of Manning, northeast corner of the intersection). The basement of that school was prone to becoming a swimming pool in wet weather. Not that this was an unheard-of condition in rural school basements, mind you. The solution, however, was typical, pure Iowa neighborhood know-how. Several of the fathers simply got together and hand-dug a ditch to a creek not far away and laid a line of drainage tile. And that, as they say, was that. No fuss, no passing the buck, just get it done. The kids needed an education.

The Colors of Fall
Rural Schools II

It had been a restful summer, but now there were things that needed to be done. The rural school teacher had been in contact with the county superintendent's office. She knew what procedural changes would be in effect this year. She had received a list of approved textbooks for the various grades and subjects, and she now had a schedule of the monthly film dates. The next step was to contact the families.

So it was that Golda Sander, teacher of Ewoldt No. 2, drove onto our farm place that August evening. It was an exciting event, because all grumbling to the contrary, we really did like school. It wasn't a long visit - simply a few minutes to greet the family, give some information about the beginning of school, and bring the parents the textbook list.

These were the days before free textbooks. Each family was given a list of the books their child would need for the various subjects. The parents would then purchase those books at their own expense at Lewis-Reinhold drug in Manning. The drug store, one of Manning's most durable Main Street businesses, was the official textbook outlet for the rural schools.

So the Graus and the Genzens, the Musfeldts and the Middendorfs, the Hansens and all the other families over the years headed for the drug store to purchase the schoolbooks, their foundation for another year of learning.

But this was not the only stop in the back-to-school shopping trip. From the drug store the path led directly to the Dime Store (Ben Franklin Store at the time) for other necessities. No desk was complete without a Big Chief tablet, several new pencils, and a new box of Crayola crayons. (Nobody really called them "crayons" in our neighborhood. They were simply a new box of "colors".)

Other stops might be made at Clifford Johnson's shoe store, Schelldorf's (or later Beisch's) clothing store, or Manning's department store, J. M. McDonald (often referred to as Brown-McDonald's). School wardrobes, which were sparse by 21st century standards, included one or two new pairs of overalls, corduroy pants or jeans for the boys, perhaps a new dress for the girls, and sometimes a new pair of shoes. In many homes, school clothes arrived by mail in boxes with the return address of Montgomery Ward or Sears Roebuck. Catalog purchases of clothing were common as was the practice of making clothes on the home sewing machine. More than one boy or girl went proudly to school wearing something new lovingly sewn by their mother out of material from an old flour sack.

Back home after school shopping, the treasures were placed together in readiness for the first day of school. What excitement and anticipation! New clothes were tried on several times, just for effect. The new books were carefully opened to reveal the mysteries in store for the coming months, and the crayons were inspected ... over and over again. Their aroma of newness carried a sense of tomorrow and of promise. It was, after all, a time of new beginning. But as sweet as the smell of new clothes, and as exciting was the musty, papery smell of new books, the real aroma was found when one opened a new box of colors. It was as if all the possibilities of life, and the pictures that could be drawn, were condensed into that little green and yellow box. To this day, nothing can carry this writer back to Ewoldt No. 2 and his childhood like a new box of colors.

A Fine Beginning
Rural Schools III

What a buzz! What excitement!

It took very little urging to get us up this morning. The tinge of chill in the late summer air got us moving and dressed in a hurry. Those new clothes had waited long enough to be worn. Mothers placed breakfast onto farmhouse tables, but there would be no dawdling over cereal or eggs or pancakes this day. This was the first day of school!

The cars and pickups stopped at the edge of the graveled road spilling excited children into the ditch along the school yard. Chatter was everywhere as classmates greeted each other and parents exchanged hellos over the murmur of idling engines. They wouldn't visit too long, as there were still farm chores waiting at home. A few words with a neighbor or a greeting of the teacher, however, were pleasant opportunities not to be passed by.

It was all new and fresh, familiar and old. The swings, the sandbox and the turning bar were all there - just like last year. The desks, attached in rows to long "sled runners" of wood, were there with the familiar initials scratched into some of the tops. Each of us hoped to move to a larger desk than we had last year.

The black metal lunch pails with white adhesive tape name labels were lined up on the shelves in the hallway. The crockery water cooler stood on the low table with some of the children's water glasses placed nearby. (Most of the glasses were extra table glasses brought from home, but some lucky kids had those pop-out metal ones.)

Nine o'clock. Mrs. Sander was ringing the little bell. We each found a desk. Pleasant View School was in session for another year.

Technically and officially, we were Ewoldt (Township) No. 2. We were one of the numerous rural schools placed nearly every two miles in any direction throughout western Iowa. In addition, we had a name which seemed very appropriate on this glorious fall morning - Pleasant View School.

Today even the textbooks were exciting. As we worked our way through the newest adventures of Dick, Jane, Sally, Spot, and Puff or struggled to match the perfect handwriting samples in the little writing books, we were happy to be together again. Those were different times. Even though our farms were within two miles of each other, we had not seen one another often during the summer. Some of us had not seen each other at all for those three months. In today's world that seems impossible, but daily visiting or playing with the kids down the block or even one half mile down the road was not universally done in the country. Therefore we were all ready for some serious playtime during recess.

What to play first - "Andy over," cowboys and Indians, tag, "slide down the bank," walk fence, or that old standby, boys chase the girls? None of the above. For the first recess of fall, we just walked around the school ground. We looked, talked, and rediscovered. We made ourselves at home.

Back inside for arithmetic. It was sort of fun when we were little, but not so much fun later. Lower grade arithmetic books had new things inside; upper grade ones had *work*. Those big red arithmetic books for upper grades contained long division and long addition columns. (I never did figure out what the dickens "adding endings" meant until I was a Manning High School senior keeping the home book at basketball games. With two coaches and two referees all breathing down my neck and impatiently awaiting statistics, I finally learned what that addition shortcut was all about.). The big red arithmetic books also came equipped with big blue drill books with pages and pages of drill problems. It was enough to make an eighth grade boy weep ... or draw pictures instead.

Noon. The black lunch pails came open as we sat outside and ate our dinner. The terms "lunch" and "dinner" have gotten somewhat confused in our modern day. Back then it was "dinner." The pails contained whole tomatoes, boiled eggs, carrots, and other farm fare beside the typical sandwich. In winter, milk was replaced by hot soup and cocoa. Occasionally the glass thermos bottle liner exploded as the top was opened mixing cold air and hot liquids.

The day passed, and then it was time to go home. Most of us walked the mile or so after school in good weather. The Genzens and Betty Lengemann, the Grau and the Spies kids headed south. The Handlos and the Singsank kids headed east. The Musfeldts and Hansens, the Muhlbauers, the Rohes and the Stribes headed north. Sheryl Hill went west.

Over the years the names changed, but the pattern remained. The crunch of gravel underfoot, the pungent, dusty smell of dry fall vegetation along the roadside, the waves and goodbyes, the turning around to watch the heads disappear over the hill until the next day. It was a fine beginning to a very good year.

We Were a Little Family
Rural Schools IV

There's no real way to describe the experience of attending a rural school except by means of impressions. The memories really aren't always that clear and precise; they're more like dim images of an old movie. There are sights, sounds, and smells, but all is slightly out of focus.

There are no sharp images, but if I close my eyes I can almost smell that fall mixture of summer-empty-schoolhouse mustiness mixed with fresh floor oil, new colors, school books, pencil sharpener shavings, dust from the gravel roads, dry grass, and the pungent odor of the outhouses.

Nothing is distinct, but if I listen closely I can hear leather-soled shoes on the wood floors, the metal slap of the desk seats being folded up against the desk behind, the rattle of metal and glass as someone plays with an inkwell, the squeak of the swing chains against the iron pipe that held them, the tap and scratch of chalk against the slate blackboards, the snap of the flag and the ring of the flag clips against the pole, the clunk of a metal lunch pail tossed upon the hallway shelf, and the glassy rattle of the library cabinet door being closed.

Though years have passed, I can feel the excitement of the first day of school, the cold wind that whipped around the northwest corner of the building during the winter, the cool hardness of the concrete storm cellar ceiling with its metal manhole cover where we'd sit and talk, the sharp stab of splinters from sliding down the basement trap door or wild rose thorns from sliding down the roadside bank, and the thrill of making it past that slanty part when we walked the top rail of the school yard fence during recess.

The image is dim, but I can still see that old globe suspended from the ceiling pulleys with sash cord and balanced with a sash weight, that big picture of George Washington that hung on the back wall, the stacked orange crates which became a room divider for that little reading and play corner in the back of the room, those old canvas window shades hanging in sets (one to go up, one to go down), the earthen dam/walkway constructed across the ditch by the students with such precision that the county had to get a bulldozer to dig it out, the games of cowboys and Indians that spilled over into the surrounding cornfield, the basement coal room, and the newly installed electric lights that allowed us to keep the same school schedule during the fall, winter, and spring.

And then there were the special events like Thanksgiving dinners, Christmas programs, a train ride to Carroll, the end of the year picnic, and Valentine's parties.

There really is no way to adequately describe the experience. All school days are special in the memory of nostalgic adults, but perhaps my mother said it best, "We were a little family." We didn't have a whole town surrounding our school - just gravel roads, fields, and sky. There weren't very many of us, usually fewer than 20 in the whole school. We weren't world-wise or street-smart, just farm kids who knew enough to stay out of the pasture with the bull. That school was not only our place of learning, but it was also our social life, our neighborhood, and truly an extended family.

At the risk of embarrassing a former schoolmate, it was a couple (or several) years out of high school when I stopped to visit Stan Spies who was working at an implement company on the west side of town. We kind of caught up on what each of us had been doing lately, and Stan folded us both up with an account of his attempt to weld a used gasoline tank. (Children, do not try this at home.) After a good laugh at ourselves and our attempts to do what no man had ever done before, we kind of stood there in silence for a couple of minutes. We really didn't have to talk right then. We had grown up together in that little rural school. We were sort of family. Nothing more needed to be said.

AUTHOR'S NOTE: This series on rural school experiences has been over a year in the making. I wish to pay tribute to some Manning friends who served as sources of memories and information regarding the rural schools. Special thanks to Dale Vollstedt, Russell Spies, Linda Ahrendsen, Betty (Lengemann) Andresen, Clifford Tank, my mother Ida Musfeldt, and all those who shared stories about that grand educational institution - the rural school.

Much more could be said and many memories could be shared between former rural school students.

This being written during the year we will gather for our all-school high school reunion, it is fitting to remember Manning High where most of us from the rural schools finally wound up. That was the place that pulled us all together and made us a real community.

It would be interesting, however, to have a rural school reunion or celebration some time. Back in the years when the rural population was so much larger than now, those schools were the place where the children and grandchildren of German and Scandinavian immigrant farmers took their first steps toward a future in their new homeland.